Welcome to Penhally Bay!

Nestled on the rugged Cornish coast is the picturesque town of Penhally. With sandy beaches, breathtaking landscapes and a warm, bustling community—it is the lucky tourist who stumbles upon this little haven.

But now Mills & Boon® Medical™ Romance is giving readers the unique opportunity to visit this fictional coastal town through our brand-new twelve-book continuity… You are welcomed to a town where the fishing boats bob up and down in the bay, surfers wait expectantly for the waves, friendly faces line the cobbled streets and romance flutters on the Cornish sea breeze…

We introduce you to Penhally Bay Surgery, where you can meet the team led by caring and commanding Dr Nick Tremayne. Each book will bring you an emotional, tempting romance—from Mediterranean heroes to a sheikh with a guarded heart. There's royal scandal that leads to marriage for a baby's sake, and handsome playboys are tamed by their blushing brides! Top-notch city surgeons win adoring smiles from the community, and little miracle babies will warm your hearts. But that's not all…

With Penhally Bay you get double the reading pleasure… as each book also follows the life of damaged hero Dr Nick Tremayne. His story will pierce your heart—a tale of lost love and the torment of forbidden romance. Dr Nick's unquestionable, unrelenting skill would leave any patient happy in the knowledge that she's in safe hands, and is a testament to the ability and dedication of all the staff at Penhally Bay Surgery. Come in and meet them for yourself…

Dear Reader

This book is a triply lovely one for me. Firstly, I was so thrilled to be asked to take part in the **Brides of Penhally Bay** series, as one of our best ever family holidays was spent in Cornwall and I have fantastic memories of the area. Secondly, it means I'm part of a very special year—because Mills & Boon is 100 years old this year. I'm so proud to be part of their history. And thirdly…I've wanted to write a vet book with a vet heroine for *ages*. (I wanted to be a vet when I was little.) So when my editor talked to me about the book, I was delighted!

There are lots of things I love about this book. I love the fact that my heroine is a princess in disguise. I love the fact that Dragan, my hero, is incredibly brave and incredibly private—and my heroine's the one who cracks open the fortress round his heart. I love Dragan's dog (who's based on a real-life Flatcoat Retriever called Bramble, borrowed from fellow author Margaret McDonagh). I love the warmth of the community in Penhally. And I really had a ball chatting with my other author friends, talking over secondary characters. (I was also forced to try out a farm shop's ice cream and cheese with Medical™ author Caroline Anderson. Research is terribly hard work…)

If you enjoy reading this even one per cent as much as I enjoyed writing this, then you're in for a real treat. Of course, because it's one of mine, you'll need a box of tissues handy. But I guarantee you'll be smiling at the end. (And watch out for the parrot—borrowed from fellow author Maggie Kingsley.)

I'm always delighted to hear from readers, so do come and visit me at www.katehardy.com

With love

Kate Hardy

THE DOCTOR'S ROYAL LOVE-CHILD

BY
KATE HARDY

MILLS & BOON®
Pure reading pleasure

For Sheila, my wonderful editor

First published in Great Britain 2008
Harlequin Mills & Boon Limited,
Eton House, 18-24 Paradise Road, Richmond, Surrey TW9 1SR

© Pamela Brooks 2008

ISBN: 978 0 263 19867 6

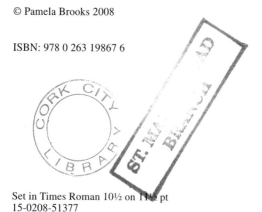

Set in Times Roman 10½ on 11½ pt
15-0208-51377

Printed and bound in Great Britain
by Antony Rowe Ltd, Chippenham, Wiltshire

Kate Hardy lives on the outskirts of Norwich with her husband, two small children, a dog—and too many books to count! She wrote her first book at age six, when her parents gave her a typewriter for her birthday. She had the first of a series of sexy romances published at twenty-five, and swapped a job in marketing communications for freelance health journalism when her son was born, so she could spend more time with him. She's wanted to write for Mills & Boon since she was twelve—and when she was pregnant with her daughter, her husband pointed out that writing Medical™ Romances would be the perfect way to combine her interest in health issues with her love of good stories.

Kate is always delighted to hear from readers—do drop in to her website at www.katehardy.com

Recent titles by this author:

THE DOCTOR'S VERY SPECIAL CHRISTMAS
THE ITALIAN GP'S BRIDE
THE CONSULTANT'S NEW-FOUND FAMILY

Did you know that Kate Hardy also writes for Modern™ Extra? Some recent titles include:

ONE NIGHT, ONE BABY
BREAKFAST AT GIOVANNI'S
IN THE GARDENER'S BED

BRIDES OF PENHALLY BAY
Bachelor doctors become husbands and fathers—
in a place where hearts are made whole.

**At Christmas we met pregnant doctor Lucy Tremayne
when she was reunited with the man she loves**
Christmas Eve Baby by Caroline Anderson

**Then in January we snuggled up for some much needed
winter warmth with gorgeous Italian doctor Marco Avanti**
The Italian's New-Year Marriage Wish by Sarah Morgan

**February saw Adam and Maggie on a 24-hour rescue
mission where romance blossomed as the sun started to set**
The Doctor's Bride by Sunrise by Josie Metcalfe

**Single dad Jack Tremayne found a mother for his
little boy—and a bride for himself in March**
The Surgeon's Fatherhood Surprise by Jennifer Taylor

**This month there's a princess in Penhally
when HRH Melinda Fortesque comes to the Bay**
The Doctor's Royal Love-Child by Kate Hardy

Edward Tremayne finds the woman of his dreams in May
Nurse Bride, Bayside Wedding by Gill Sanderson

**Meet hunky Penhally Bay Chief Inspector Lachlan D'Ancey
and follow his search for love this June**
Single Dad Seeks a Wife by Melanie Milburne

**The temperature really hots up in July when devastatingly
handsome Dr Oliver Fawkner arrives in the Bay…**
Virgin Midwife, Playboy Doctor by Margaret McDonagh

**Curl up with Francesca and Mark in August as they
try one last time for the baby they've always longed for...**
Their Miracle Baby by Caroline Anderson

**September brings sexy Sheikh Zayed
from his desert kingdom to the beaches of Penhally**
Sheikh Surgeon Claims His Bride by Josie Metcalfe

Snuggle up with dishy Dr Tom Cornish in October
A Baby for Eve by Maggie Kingsley

**And don't miss French doctor Pierre,
who sweeps into the Bay this November**
Dr Devereux's Proposal by Margaret McDonagh

A collection to treasure for ever!

CHAPTER ONE

'FANCY seeing you here, Dr Lovak,' Melinda said with a grin as Dragan wound down the window of his car. 'Anyone would think I had matched my call lists to yours.'

Knowing that she'd done exactly that when she'd phoned him after her morning's surgery—except his first call had taken a little longer than he'd expected, which was why he was arriving at the boarding kennels just as she was leaving—Dragan smiled back. 'Tut-tut, Ms Fortesque. Suggest things like that and people might start to talk.'

'If they do, I'll just tell them I wanted to check on my favourite patient and see how her leg's doing. Isn't that right, Bramble?' Melinda looked over Dragan's shoulder at the flatcoat retriever they'd rescued a few months before, who was lying on a blanket in the back of his car.

The dog's tail thumped loudly, and she gave a soft answering woof.

'Hear that? Bramble says she'll be my alibi.' Melinda leaned in through the open window and stole a kiss from Dragan. 'Though I think people might have already started to guess, *amore mio*. Do you know how many people this last month have told me what a wonderful doctor you are?'

'Funny, that. People have been singing your praises to me, too.' He stole a kiss right back. 'But that's the thing about living in a place like Penhally. Everybody knows everything about everyone.' Or nearly everything. So, despite the fact that they'd kept their relationship low-key, he was pretty sure that everybody in Penhally knew that the vet and the doctor were an item.

For a moment, he could've sworn that worry flashed into Melinda's gorgeous blue eyes. But then the expression was gone again. No, he must be imagining things. What did Melinda have to hide, anyway? She'd come to England on holiday years ago, had fallen in love with the country and decided to settle here and train to be a vet.

Not so very different from himself. Although holidays had been the last thing on his mind when he'd walked off that boat seventeen years ago, he too had fallen in love with England. And he was as settled here in Cornwall as he'd ever be anywhere. The wild Atlantic wasn't quite the same as the Adriatic, but at least the sound of the sea could still lull him to sleep at night.

'Do you have time for lunch?' she asked.

He shook his head. 'Sorry. I'm already behind schedule. And I really can't keep my patients waiting.'

'Of course you can't.' She stroked his cheek. 'I'll cook for us tonight, then. Your place.'

He turned his head to press a kiss into her palm. 'That would be lovely. Though you don't have to cook for me, Melinda. I'm perfectly capable of doing it.'

She scoffed and put her hands on her hips, shaking her head at him as he got out of the car. 'Dragan Lovak, you know as well as I do that you *never* cook. That if I let you, you'd live on bread and cheese and cold meats and salad—even in the middle of winter.'

He flapped a dismissive hand. 'Well. Food doesn't have to be hot. It's fuel.'

'It's much more than that,' she told him. 'You don't just shovel down calories like a Ferrari taking on petrol at a pit stop. Food is a *pleasure*. Something to be enjoyed.'

Since Melinda had been in his life, Dragan was beginning to appreciate that. Not only because she was a fantastic cook: her enjoyment of food had taught him to notice flavour. Texture. Aroma. Things he'd blocked out in the dark days and that he'd more or less trained himself to ignore since then. 'Are you on call tonight?' he asked.

'No. It's the turn of the other practice to cover tonight. What about you?'

'No. And I'm not on late surgery, either.'

'So we have the whole evening to ourselves. *Bene.*' Her eyes sparkled. 'I'll pick up something at the Trevellyans' farm shop and bring it over to cook when I've finished surgery, yes?'

Recently she'd spent more nights at his little terraced cottage in Fisherman's Row than at her own flat above the veterinary surgery, just round the corner. Maybe, Dragan thought, it was time that he gave Melinda her own key. Time that they took their relationship to the next level. Time that he asked her to move in with him.

Though it was taking one hell of a risk. Since his family had been killed during the war in Croatia, he'd kept people at a distance—just close enough to be polite and pleasant and easy to work with, but far enough away to keep his heart safe. He reasoned that if he didn't let people too close, he wouldn't get hurt if he lost them, or if they walked away.

He'd kept his private life extremely private—until Melinda Fortesque had entered his life. With just one smile, the Italian vet had cracked the fortress round his heart wide open, and she'd walked straight in.

But although part of him wanted it so badly—to ask her to live with him, be his love, make a new family with him— the fear flooded in and stopped the words before he could say them. What if it all went wrong? What if he lost her? He didn't think he'd be able to pick up the pieces again. Not this time.

He shivered.

'Dragan? You are cold?'

On a sunny spring day like this? Hardly. He summoned a smile. 'No. I'm…' No. This wasn't the right time or the right place for that particular discussion. 'Late for my appointment,' he finished wryly. 'I'll see you later.'

'OK. *Ciao.*' She blew him a kiss. '*Zlato.*'

His mouth must have dropped open, because she laughed. 'You're not the only one who can speak several languages, you know.'

Italian was Melinda's native tongue and he knew she also spoke French and Spanish as well as English, albeit with a slight Italian accent.

But she'd just called him 'darling' in his own tongue.

Croatian.

How many years had it been since he'd heard that word spoken?

'Dragan?' She was looking worried. 'What's the matter? I said it wrong—it doesn't mean what I think it means and I've just mortally insulted you?'

'No.' He forced himself to smile. 'You said it perfectly. I wasn't expecting it, that's all.' And it had brought back memories he usually kept locked away.

She shook her head. 'I can see it in your eyes. I hurt you. I didn't mean to—'

'Hey.' He got out of the car and slid his arms round her, held her close. Rested his cheek against her soft, silky hair and breathed in the sweet scent he always associated with her. 'I know you didn't, *piccola mia.* It's all right.'

'I looked it up on the internet. How to say "*amore mio*" in Croatian. I just wanted to…well, to please you,' she said softly.

'You did. You *do.*' He was so close to telling her how much she meant to him. How he really felt about her. Just how much he loved her. But the first time he said those words, he wanted it to be perfect. Romantic. At the top of the cliffs, with moonlight shining over the Atlantic—or maybe at sunrise. A new dawn, a new beginning. He hadn't quite worked out the details. But the middle of the car park of the local boarding kennels really wasn't the right place for a declaration of love.

Especially when he was supposed to be working. And so was she.

He let her go. 'I'll see you later. Have a nice afternoon.'

She lifted herself on tiptoe and kissed him. 'You, too.'

The touch of her mouth against his made him forget his good intentions. He wrapped his arms round her again, let the kiss deepen. Lost himself in the warmth and sweetness of her mouth.

Until a polite cough interrupted them.

'My apologies,' he said to Lizzie Chamberlain, the owner of the boarding kennels. 'I, um…' What could he say? He was meant to be here to check on her mother and talk about the consultant's report she'd just received. Yet here he was, kissing the vet stupid in the middle of the car park.

Lizzie just smiled. 'It's nice to see you both looking so happy.'

Melinda's face was bright red and his felt as if it were a matching shade. And he couldn't think of a single word to say.

Luckily Melinda's brain cells seemed to snap in a little more quickly than his. '*Grazie*,' she said.

'We've thought for a while that you two were more than just good friends,' Lizzie commented. 'But you kept everyone guessing.'

Melinda's fingers twined around Dragan's. 'It's very new,' she said softly. 'Dragan and I…we both like a quiet life.'

'And you want time to get to know each other properly without the village grapevine interfering and people asking you when we're going to hear the bells at St Mark's,' Lizzie guessed.

'*Essattamente.*' Melinda beamed at her. 'I knew you would understand. Thank you, Lizzie. We appreciate your kindness in keeping it to yourself.' Her fingers tightened briefly round Dragan's, and then she let his hand go. 'I need to go and see a man about a dog.'

She meant it literally as well, Dragan knew; he liked her sense of humour.

Melinda smiled. '*Ciao.*' And then she was gone.

'She's such a lovely girl,' Lizzie said as Melinda drove out of the car park. 'And a brilliant vet. She's got such an affinity with animals.'

'So she was here because you're worried about one of your rescue dogs?' Dragan asked.

'A kitten, actually.'

He blinked. 'A kitten—*here*?'

'You know Polly, who helps me in the mornings? Her son Jamie was out with his friends last night when he heard this tiny mewing sound at the side of the road. They spent half an hour searching with the lights from their bikes and their mobile phones, and they found the kitten. Tiny little thing— about three weeks old, Melinda reckons. It was dehydrated, had a terrible cut on its head and its nose was rubbed raw. Jamie didn't think the vet would come out at that time of night, so he brought it over to me.' She smiled. 'Melinda said I did the right thing. Washed the cut out, fed the kitten with a dropper and nursed it for most of last night.'

'And Melinda thinks the kitten will pull through?'

'With good nursing and a bit of luck, yes.'

'Jamie brought the kitten to the right place, then,' Dragan said. Lizzie's work with rescue dogs was legendary in the area, and he was sure she'd give the kitten the attention it needed. And Melinda, no doubt, would find the kitten a home.

Just as she'd done when they'd rescued Bramble, just before Christmas. Despite being bitten, Melinda had made a fuss of the dog, calmed her down and then taken her into Theatre and set to work fixing the dog's broken leg.

Lizzie smiled. 'Your Melinda's wonderful, you know. She's so good with people. Since she's let Tina help her out on Saturday mornings, there's been a world of difference in her attitude—I don't get those surly teenage grunts and glares any more, and she does her homework without complaining. Your Melinda's taught her a lot—she's given Tina the time the teachers just can't nowadays and answered all her questions. And she's lent Tina some books about poultry since Turbo Chick arrived.' The chick had got its name because it was enormous and nobody believed it could possibly have come out of an ordinary chicken's egg— except Tina had been videoing the eggs as part of a school project and had actually filmed the chick bursting out. 'She's a gem.'

His Melinda.

Funny how that phrase made him feel all warm and fuzzy inside. A feeling he'd never thought to have again. Dragan smiled. 'I don't suppose I could persuade you that we're just good friends.'

'After seeing you kiss her like that?' Lizzie teased. 'And you've changed, too. You've smiled a lot more since she came to the village.'

Dragan raised an eyebrow. 'My name's pronounced Dra-*gahn*, not Dragon.'

Lizzie laughed. 'You know what I mean. Mum adores you but she worries that you're a little too quiet. Too serious.'

'But if I started roaring around on a motorbike or bought a Maserati like Marco had, or wore trendy clothes and had my ear pierced, everyone would say I was having a midlife crisis,' Dragan said with a smile.

'I think,' Lizzie said, 'if you started roaring round on a motorbike, you'd have all the teenage girls in the village mooning over you.'

He laughed it off. 'Flattery. At thirty-five, I'm practically double their age. Much too old.' Then he sobered. 'Before we go in to see Stella—how is she really, Lizzie?'

Lizzie grimaced. 'Up and down. Sometimes she's bright and interested in what's going on. Other days, it takes her an hour to get dressed, she can barely walk from the sitting room to the kitchen, and you can hardly understand a word she says.'

Dragan nodded. 'I had the consultant's report through yesterday.' It was the reason he was doing a house call today—to discuss it with Lizzie and Stella, knowing that Stella would find it hard to get down into the village and Lizzie simply couldn't drop everything and ferry her mother about. 'It annoys me when these consultants think they have to write in medical jargon all the time. Especially when they're sending their report to a patient. I know they have to be accurate because they worry about lawsuits, but this is ridiculous.' He shook his head in exasperation. 'I swear they'd call a spade "an implement for displacing an admixture of organic remains".'

'I did look some of it up,' Lizzie admitted. 'But "hypophonia" was beyond me.'

'It means the voice is very quiet—"phonia" refers to the voice and "hypo" means "under". Literally, under-voicing. Stella's pronouncing her words properly, not slurring them, or they would have called it "dysphonia". It's the volume that's the problem,' Dragan explained.

'And "retropulsion"?'

'Movement backwards. They're concerned about how easy Stella finds it to walk or move about. That was the test where they asked her to walk forwards and backwards along a line, yes?'

Lizzie nodded, looking worried. 'The consultant said that I should think about Mum's care needs. But we've had the occupational therapy team out and they said there wasn't much more that they could do. They've put grab rails in her bedroom and the bathroom and a seat on the bath, and they've raised the level of her chair so she can get out of it more easily.' She bit her lip. 'I don't want her going into a home. She's my mum and I want to look after her.'

'Nobody's saying she has to go into a home,' Dragan said gently. 'But I did notice what the psychologist said in the report about the mood swings—as you know, depression's common in Parkinson's.'

'But she's not going mad.'

'Of course she's not,' Dragan said. 'That bit about perceptual problems means she doesn't necessarily see things how they really are. Which can be a strain on you.'

'I'm fine,' Lizzie said.

He wasn't so sure. Lizzie's smile was a little too bright for his liking. 'I think that the odd bit of respite care might help you both. A morning at a day centre once a week, where Stella would get a chance to make some new friends and have some outside interests and have some fun—and it would give you a break, too, a few hours where you don't have to worry about your mum as well as everything else.'

'I'm fine,' Lizzie repeated, shaking her head. 'No need to worry about me.'

'You've got a lot on your plate, Lizzie—and, yes, you do it brilliantly, but even Wonder Woman would have days when she struggled with *your* workload,' Dragan said softly. 'Running a business—and not just any old business either, because you do the rescue work with the dogs as well as the boarding kennels—plus bringing up Tina on your own and being a full-time carer to your mum…It's an awful lot to ask of someone.'

'I manage.'

'I know. You more than manage. But I also want you to know that you don't have to do it all on your own. The help's there whenever you need it. I'm not going to push you into something you don't want, but I also don't want to see you struggle when you don't have to.' He squeezed her shoulder. 'Don't be too proud.'

'Are you bringing Bramble in? Mum'd like to see her.'

He noticed the change of subject, but he realised that now wasn't the right time to push Lizzie. He'd deliberately parked in the shade—as he always did when he took Bramble on house calls—but some of his patients liked to see the dog, including Stella Chamberlain. And there was evidence that petting an animal helped to lower blood pressure and increase the general well-being of patients. His ready agreement to Lizzie's suggestion had nothing to do with the fact that he loved having a dog again and hated being parted from Bramble.

Much.

'Come on, girl.' He opened the boot of his estate car, and lifted the dog out so she wouldn't bang her injured leg. He knew he was being overprotective, but the leg had been slow to heal and he didn't want to take any risks.

Stella was delighted to see Bramble and made a huge fuss of her. Though Dragan could see that she was having one of her 'off' days—she was definitely struggling to get out of the chair, despite the fact the legs had been raised, and by the end of every sentence her voice was so soft that he could barely hear her. She listened intently to what he had to say about the consultant's report and the changes in her medication to help with the stiffness in her gait and her memory lapses, but Stella, like Lizzie, completely rejected the idea of day care.

'I'm not spending my days stuck in a home with a load of daft old bats. This is where I live, and this is where I'm staying,' Stella said, lifting her chin.

'You won't be stuck anywhere. It's a...' He struggled to think of something that might entice Stella. 'A bit like a coffee morning where you sit and chat, or you have someone to give a demonstration of something and you all have a go afterwards.'

'I don't want to sit and chat with people I don't know,' Stella insisted.

Time to back off. 'It's just a suggestion. Nobody's going to force you to do anything you don't want to do,' Dragan reassured her.

'Good. Because I'm *not* going.'

Maybe he'd talk to Melinda, Dragan thought. Not about Stella's condition—he would never break patient confidentiality—but she was good with people. She'd got Tina to open up to her, confide her dreams of becoming a vet, and had then talked to George about giving the teenager some work experience at the practice. Perhaps Melinda would have some ideas about how to persuade Stella and Lizzie that a weekly session of day care could help them both. Because, the way things were going here, he could see Lizzie ending up having a breakdown.

'Remember, call me any time you need to,' he said to Lizzie as he lifted Bramble back into the car. 'That's what I'm here for.'

'I will.'

Though he knew she wouldn't. She'd straighten her backbone and just carry on.

He took his leave, then headed out to see his next patient.

CHAPTER TWO

DRAGAN had been home half an hour when the doorbell rang. Bramble barked—just in case he'd missed the fact someone was on the doorstep—and pattered behind him as he opened the door.

'Dinner will be approximately thirty minutes,' Melinda announced, holding up two brown paper bags.

Not take-away food either, Dragan knew as he followed her into his kitchen. Melinda liked to cook from scratch.

'First of all, this needs to go into the freezer.' She retrieved a tub of ice cream from one of the bags and put it in the coldest part of the freezer. 'And next, for you, because you're beautiful.' She bent down and made a fuss of the dog, then took a handful of treats from her pocket and fed them to Bramble one by one.

From the blur of her wagging tail, Dragan knew that the dog loved having Melinda around as much as he did. 'You spoil that dog,' he remarked.

'And you don't?' she teased.

'Never,' he deadpanned. 'So where's my treat, then?'

She grinned, reached up and slid her arms round his neck, then kissed him thoroughly. 'Better?'

He smiled. 'Much better. Want a hand making dinner?'

'Absolutely not.' She shook her head. 'It's wonderful being

able to work in a proper kitchen. The one in the flat over the surgery isn't even big enough for a hamster wheel.'

And she looked good in his kitchen, he thought. At home. So much so that she didn't hesitate to switch on his iPod and pick out some of the tracks she liked, by an opera-pop crossover artist that she'd downloaded for him the previous week. He'd never heard of the singer before, but he liked it, especially when she was singing along to it, half humming and half singing the lyrics. She was as good with the Spanish lyrics as she was with the Italian ones, and he loved the sweetness of her voice.

It wasn't just the music. He loved having her around, full stop.

Because she made his house feel like *home*. She had done ever since her second visit to the cottage, when she'd brought him the iPod, complete with a set of speakers for his kitchen, and insisted that he accepted the gift. 'You can't cook properly without music, Dragan. You can't *live* without music.'

Melinda was always singing. And she always took over the CD player in his car. Since she'd been around, there had been a lot more music in his life.

A lot more everything.

Maybe he'd ask her tonight. Maybe he'd take her for a walk on the beach and kiss her under the stars and ask her to stay. For always.

He enjoyed just watching her as she chopped and stirred and tasted and stirred a bit more.

Then she looked over at him and the corners of her eyes crinkled. 'You can lay the table, if you like.'

The small bistro table was set in front of the French doors that overlooked the garden; although it wasn't like the huge rambling garden he'd grown up with, he enjoyed his little patch of green. Right now it was full of spring flowers, with a carpet of blue squill underneath the apple tree. He set the table, took a bottle of white wine from the fridge, poured two glasses, and sat down as she brought over two plates.

Bramble immediately settled on the floor between the two of them, and Melinda laughed. 'Ah, no, you can't have any of this, *bellissima*. The chilli sauce won't be kind to your stomach.'

'And she's already wolfed down half a dozen prawns while you were preparing this,' Dragan pointed out.

'Of course. She's my official tester.' Melinda waited until he'd taken his first mouthful of the avocado with prawns and chilli sauce. 'So do you like it?'

'It's fabulous,' he said honestly. Trust Melinda to come up with a combination he would never have thought of.

The lemon chicken with broccoli, carrots and new potatoes was equally good. And although he didn't have a sweet tooth, he was content to watch her eat the hazelnut meringue ice cream that was a speciality of the Trevellyans' farm shop and which she absolutely adored.

'So you admit now that food is not just fuel?' Melinda demanded when they cleared the table together.

'Yes, I admit it. You are right and I am wrong, *carissima*.'

She laughed. 'And therefore you owe me a forfeit.'

He laughed back. 'Indeed. It's in the cupboard next to the fridge.' He never ate chocolate, but Melinda loved it, so he'd taken to buying some just for her. Rich, dark chocolate flavoured with spices and a hint of orange.

She found the bar of chocolate within seconds. 'For someone who never touches the stuff, you have amazingly good taste, Dr Lovak.'

Her little 'oh' of pleasure as she snapped off the first square and slid it into her mouth sent desire flickering down his spine. A desire he could see matched in her beautiful blue eyes.

He made them both coffee, strong and dark, and placed the mugs on his low coffee-table before sitting on the sofa and pulling her onto his lap. He loved having her near. And he loved it even more when she kissed him spontaneously, cupping his face and nibbling at his lower lip to deepen the kiss. He loved the silky feel of her hair against his skin, her sweet floral scent, the warmth of her body against his.

He tipped her back on the sofa and was halfway through undoing her shirt when she groaned. 'Dragan. You should've been born in Sparta.'

'What?' He frowned. 'I'm not with you.'

'Your *sofa*. It's like a bed of nails.'

It wasn't the most comfortable in the world, true, but it did him. He didn't actually spend much time on it anyway—he was either out walking with the dog or somewhere with Melinda or sitting at the little table, working on some notes on his laptop. He smiled and stroked her hair back from her face. 'Don't be such a princess.'

She stiffened, then pushed him away and sat up, buttoning her shirt again.

He frowned. 'Melinda? What's wrong?'

'Nothing.' Her face shuttered. 'I ought to be going.'

What? A few seconds ago they'd been kissing. Undressing each other—she'd completely unbuttoned his own shirt. And now she'd gone all frosty on him. He couldn't think of anything he'd done wrong. 'What? Why? Neither of us is on call. I thought we were spending time together?' Then the penny dropped. He'd accused her of being princessy. 'This princess business—I was teasing, *tesoro*. You know the story of the princess who can still feel the tiny pea through fifty mattresses—that's like the way you complain about my sofa.'

'Uh-huh.'

He didn't understand why she was reacting so badly— Melinda had a great sense of humour usually, and it was rare for her not to have a smile on her face—but he hated the idea of her being hurt and him being the cause. He slid his arm round her and hugged her. 'You're not like that at all—you

don't have any airs and graces, and your four-by-four isn't
like that dreadful woman's next door.'

'What woman?'

'I didn't catch her name—I wasn't paying attention,' he
admitted. 'Natalie or Natasha or Na...I don't know. It's not
important.' He flapped a dismissive hand. 'She's staying next
door in the holiday cottage. Hopefully not for too long. Now,
she's the princessy type. Hair cut in the latest fashion,
designer clothes and shoes, a four-by-four that's probably
never been within a mile of an untarmacked track in its life.
Whereas yours is covered in mud outside and animal hair
inside.'

Her mouth tightened. 'So now you're saying I look a mess.'

'*No*. I'm saying you're the most beautiful woman I've ever
met, you don't need make-up to emphasise how lovely you
are and you'd manage to look stylish in a...oh, in a potato
sack.' He made an impatient gesture with his hand. 'I don't
have a clue why we're fighting—I don't want to argue with
you, Melinda.' He sighed. 'Actually, I wanted to talk to you
about something tonight.'

'What?'

'When you look as if you want to slap me?' He shook his
head. 'No way.' There was no point in asking her. She'd reject
him straight out, and then their relationship would slowly start
to fall apart.

'I don't want to slap you. But I don't like what you said.'

'Then I apologise. Without reservation.' Clearly he'd
touched a raw nerve. He had no idea why his throw-away
comment had upset her so badly; or maybe he'd accidentally
repeated something that an ex had once said to hurt her. 'I
really didn't mean to hurt you, Melinda. I'd never do that. You
mean too much to me.'

She remained perfectly still for a moment, then she
nodded, as if reassured, slid her arm round his waist and

leaned into him. 'Apology accepted. So what did you want to talk about?'

'The idea was to go for a walk. Up on the cliffs, or barefoot on the sand. In the moonlight or maybe watching the sun rise.'

She pulled a face. 'You want me to get up before dawn?'

'Yes—No.' He raked a hand through his hair distractedly. 'Melinda. Today, when you called me *zlato*—did you mean it?'

She frowned. 'Why?'

'I asked first.'

'Yes. And it upset you.'

'Only because it's been a long, long time since anyone used that word to me. Remember, I've lived in England for half my life now.'

'Didn't you ever want to go back to Croatia?'

'There's nothing there for me any more.'

His face and voice were both expressionless. And Melinda knew without a doubt that this was what haunted Dragan. What caused the shadows in his eyes. And that night she'd stayed here last month and had woken up in the middle of the night to find him standing by the window, staring out at the sea with such a bleak expression that it had almost broken her heart…He'd refused to talk about it, but she had a feeling this was to do with the same thing.

And she also had the feeling that this was the last tiny barrier between them.

Ha. As if she had the right to push him to talk, when she never talked about what had driven her to England. But how could she talk about it? She knew from experience that the minute people knew about her family, they started treating her differently. Either they withdrew from her because they secretly thought that she was just slumming it and didn't really want their friendship, or they started seeing her as a passport to high society.

Except she didn't hang out with high society. She'd never fitted in—and although her parents hadn't actually taken the step of disowning her, they didn't approve of her life here. On the rare occasions she went back to Contarini they never talked about her job, almost as if ignoring it meant that it wasn't really happening. To listen to her parents, anyone would think that she was merely living abroad for a while to broaden her life experience, and spent her days shopping and sightseeing.

Most of the time Melinda managed to put it to the back of her mind and get on with her life. And she was happy: she'd never been particularly close to her parents, she loathed her brother Raffi's playboy friends, and she had nothing in common with her sister Serena's Sloaney mates, so it didn't worry her that she was pretty much on her own here.

Whereas Dragan, she thought, was different. Like her, he felt there was nothing for him in his old home but, unlike her, he missed it and it hurt so much that it was like a fracture right across his heart—a fracture she wanted to heal.

She took his hand and pressed a kiss into it. 'Why not?'

'I'd rather not talk about it.'

'Keeping things bottled up inside isn't good for you,' she said quietly. Even though she knew she was being a hypocrite. The longer she went without telling him the secret she'd been keeping ever since she'd first come to England, the harder it was to bring up the subject—and the more scared she was about his reaction. He wasn't the social-climber type, but she really didn't want him to reject her—to see her as Princess Melinda, second in line to the throne of Contarini, instead of the girl practically next door who'd fallen in love with him.

But this wasn't about her. She pushed the thoughts away and squeezed his hand. 'You need to talk.'

'Whatever.' The flippant, dismissive drawl did nothing to disguise his pain.

'Dragan, I mean it. Talk to me.'

'There isn't much to tell.'

'Then tell me anyway.' She tightened her fingers round his. 'You trust me, don't you?' Even as she said it, she winced inwardly. A trust she hadn't given to him. But this was different. She could live with her secret because it didn't hurt her; whatever he was keeping locked inside was slowly eating him away.

'Ye-es.'

'Then tell me,' she insisted softly.

He was silent for such a long time that she didn't think he was going to talk. And then finally he spoke, his voice very low.

'We lived in a little village on the Adriatic coast. My family had a boatyard.'

She could see it in his eyes—there was more to it than that. Much more. And she guessed that the only way she'd get him to tell her was to ask questions.

'So you weren't always going to be a doctor?'

He shook his head. 'I was going into the family business when I'd finished my education.'

'Sailing boats?'

'In my spare time. My elder brother studied marine engineering and he was good with his hands—he designed and built the boats, just like my father. And I was the one who was good at languages and figures.'

She knew about the languages and could've guessed about the maths. Dragan was bright—in her view, he'd be good at absolutely anything he chose to do. 'So you would be the finance director?'

'For a while, then the idea was that I should take over from my father as managing director. He was going to retire and spend more time with my mother while he was still young enough to go out and about and enjoy their leisure time.'

She knew all about parents wanting to retire and expecting their children to take over. And she thanked God every day that she wasn't the one who'd have to take over from her father. Being a girl and being second-born meant that she'd been able to choose her life—to do the job she loved instead of one that would have stifled her. 'It sounds a good plan,' she said. Even though she had doubts about the way it would work in her own family. She'd always thought Serena, her baby sister, would make a better job of ruling than her older brother. Rafael had too much of a wild streak.

'So you were going to study economics?' she guessed.

'International law,' he said. 'In Zagreb—but I planned to spend the holidays at home in the boatyard.'

Clearly he'd loved the family business, had wanted to be part of it. He'd fitted in. Had been happy.

So what had gone wrong?

There was another long pause.

'And then the war happened.'

Five tiny words. Spoken so quietly that she could almost hear his heart breaking in the silence that followed. And all she could do was hold him. 'I'm here, *amore mio*,' she said softly.

'It wasn't just our village. It was all over the country. The fighting, the bombs, the bullets. Such a mess. Such a *waste*. Dad and I had gone to Split for a couple of days on business. Everything was fine at home when we left. And we came back to...' His breath shuddered and his jaw tightened.

She stroked his face, willing the tension to ease. Wanting him to speak. Let out the pain that was eating him away from the inside.

'Everything was gone,' he said finally, his voice flat. 'The boatyard was in ruins. My brother had been killed, my mother, the people who worked for us. All dead. And others, too, in the village. Smashed glass everywhere from the bullets. Holes ripped in buildings by bombs. And...' He swallowed. 'It's something I hope to God I never have to live through again.

I know I should be working for Doctors Without Borders. Helping people, the way I wish my own people had been helped when we needed it most. But, God help me, I just couldn't do it.' He closed his eyes. 'I'm such a selfish bastard. I couldn't bear to go back into a war zone. There are too many memories.'

'There's no "should" about it, and you're not selfish,' she told him fiercely. 'Some people want to do it—they have their own reasons for doing it. Just as you have a very good reason for *not* doing it. And you *do* help people, Dragan. You help them here. Where they need you just as much.'

'I still feel guilty.'

She kissed him gently. 'What happened wasn't your fault.'

'Not the war. But my father…' His voice trailed off.

'What happened?'

He dragged in a breath. 'The shock was too much. He collapsed. I know now it was probably a stroke, but back then my first aid was pretty basic. I could do mouth to mouth and I knew what to do if someone was drowning, but I really didn't know what to do with a heart attack or a stroke. The phones lines were out so I couldn't call an ambulance.' Back then, mobile phones hadn't been widespread, Melinda knew—that wouldn't have been an option. 'I managed to find someone with a car that could still be driven, borrowed it and took him to hospital.'

She knew from the bleakness in Dragan's eyes that his father hadn't made it.

'He died in the queue for the emergency department. And I vowed then that I'd get the medical skills. It was too late for my family, but I could stop other people losing what I'd lost.'

'Dragan, if it was a stroke, you probably couldn't have done anything for him anyway.'

His jaw tightened. 'I could've done more than I did.'

It wasn't true, but she knew that this was an argument she

wasn't going to win. And she didn't want to hurt him even more by pushing the issue and forcing him to confront it. Instead, she asked softly, 'So you went back to university, switched your course from law to medicine?'

'My father's last words to me—he told me to go to England. Where I would be safe. Where I could carry on and know my family would be proud of me, whatever I chose to do.'

'They're proud of you,' she said softly. 'I believe people still look out for you when they've passed on. Like my *nonna*—my father's mother. She supported me when I said I wanted to be a vet.' The only one of Melinda's family who'd accepted her choice of career. The only one who'd admitted that Melinda just wasn't princess material and was far happier—not to mention better at—treating sick animals than she was schmoozing with foreign dignitaries and trying to remember the finer points of etiquette. 'She died before I graduated, but I knew she was there on the day, applauding as I stepped onto the stage and accepted my degree from the chancellor of the university. And you—look at you. The village doctor. Everyone looks up to you because you're a good man and you're really good at your job. Your family are proud of you, Dragan.'

'I hope so.'

'They *are*.' She hugged him. 'So then you came here?'

'Eventually. I needed to sort out the business first.' He sighed. 'The insurance didn't cover acts of war. And there was nothing left of the boatyard. But I wasn't going to let my family name be blackened, for people to say that Lovak Marine was bankrupt and defaulted on its debts.'

She could understand that. Honour was important to Dragan. And duty.

The thought pricked her conscience: she hadn't exactly been a dutiful daughter, had she? Melinda Fortesque,

MRCVS, had chosen the much lighter responsibilities of a village vet rather than helping to shoulder the burden of running the kingdom of Contarini. Some people would see that as absconding, avoiding what she'd been born to do. 'So what did you do?'

'I sold the land. Used the proceeds to settle the mortgage and the outstanding debts.'

'And then you bought a ticket to England?'

He shook his head. 'I didn't have enough money after I'd paid the creditors, and our debtors were never going to be able to pay me what they owed. The debts had to be written off.'

Though he'd refused to let his family's debts be written off. It wasn't *fair,* Melinda thought. 'So how did you get here?'

'I bartered my way onto a ship—I would crew for them in exchange for my passage to England. And this country has been good to me, Melinda. The authorities let me stay. I had nothing—no proof of who I was, no proof that I had any qualifications in my homeland. I spent a year working as a waiter by day and studying for exams at night, until I had the qualifications I needed to study medicine.'

He'd worked his way up from nothing. Worked longer and harder than anyone else she knew. And her heart ached with pride in him. 'You're amazing,' she said softly, stroking his face. 'I don't know anyone else who would have had the strength to do all that.'

He shrugged it off. 'It wasn't that big a deal.'

Yes, it was. 'Some people, in your shoes, would be hard and bitter and never give anybody an inch. But you...you understand people. You *care*. Your family would be so proud of you. *I'm* proud of you.'

His dark eyes glittered, and he said nothing.

The strong, silent type. That was her Dragan. But now he'd opened up to her, she didn't want him to close in on himself again. 'So when you qualified, you came here?' she asked.

'I worked in London for a while. But I missed the sea. And then some friends brought me to Cornwall for the weekend. I fell in love with the area.'

'Me, too.'

'And I'm very, very glad I decided to stay. That I met you.' He rested his forehead against hers. 'I am sorry, *piccola*. I didn't mean it to get this heavy. It's not something I talk about.'

She could tell that. And how much it had stirred up his emotions. It was rare that his English slid from being perfectly accentless to having a strong Croatian accent. 'But I hope talking to me helped,' she said softly.

He brushed his mouth against hers. 'So, *zlato*. You looked up Croatian phrases on the Internet, then?'

'How else was I going to learn?'

'You could have asked me.'

'And you would have told me?'

He smiled. 'Let me teach you something now. *Volim te.*'

'What does that mean?'

'The same as *ti amo*.' He paused. 'And I do. I love you, Melinda.'

It felt as if the room were full of butterflies, the sunlight dancing on their wings. Dragan loved her. And he loved her for who she was: Melinda Fortesque, country vet.

Then the butterflies went straight into her stomach. She really ought to tell him the rest of it. He'd told her everything, and she was holding out on him. But now really wasn't the time or the place. And if she told him…would he stop loving her? Would he back away, feeling that she'd look down on him—even though she didn't?

'There was something else I wanted to say. But it's too late for sunrise.'

'Tell me anyway.'

'I've never said this to anyone else. Ever.'

'Now you're worrying me.' She kept her tone light, but fear flickered through her anyway. Had he found out about her family?

No, of course not. How could he possibly know?

But he looked so serious, so intense, that it scared her.

'I wondered…' And he tailed off.

No, no, no. She had to keep this light. Tease him out of seriousness. 'Dragan Lovak, your English is perfect—if I didn't know you came from Croatia, I'd think you *were* English. Please, don't tell me you're turning completely English on me and developing a stiff upper lip.' She fiddled with his short dark hair. 'And then this is going to go floppy and fall in your eyes. And you're going to start saying "um" a lot.'

To her relief, he smiled. And the haunted look in his eyes lessened. 'Hardly. And I'm never going to be posh anyway.'

Oh, *Dio*.

'Nothing wrong with that. I like you just how you are.' Now was definitely not the moment to tell him. Because if he was even the slightest bit worried about his background…the last thing she wanted was for him to think she was slumming it.

She'd have to work out the right way to tell him. But there was something else important he needed to know, something far more important than who she was: how she really felt about him. 'Actually, "like" is probably the wrong word.' She traced his lower lip with the pad of her forefinger. *'Volim te, zlato. Ti amo, amore mio,'* she added in her own language.

'Melinda…' He paused. 'No. It sounds wrong.'

'Try me.'

He took a deep breath. 'Move in with me.'

'Move in with you?' Now, that she hadn't been expecting.

His eyes were very dark. 'I told you it sounded wrong. Wrong time, wrong place.' He grimaced. 'I wanted to ask you somewhere romantic. "Come live with me and be my love",' that sort of thing.'

'You want me to live with you.'

'Not *just* live with me. I thought maybe we could go and talk to Reverend Kenner.'.

She blinked as what he'd just said sank in. 'You're asking me to marry you?'

'If we'd done this my way,' he pointed out, 'it'd be somewhere romantic. Not on my bed-of-nails sofa.'

'If we'd done this your way, it'd be at the crack of dawn and I wouldn't have had enough coffee to be awake enough to answer you.'

'So that's a no, then.'

'You really want to marry me?' A man who loved her for herself. A man she loved all the way back.

'Why are you so surprised? Melinda, you're like sunlight. You make everything around you seem better. And you make me a better man.'

How, when he was already a better man than she could ever wish for? 'I... Dragan, I don't know what to say.'

'I'm sorry. Forget I said anything. I'll take you home.'

'Take me home?' She stared at him, not following his logic. 'Why?'

'Because I've upset you.'

'Upset me?' She shook her head. 'How could asking me to marry you upset me? I said yes!'

'No, you didn't,' he pointed out.

'I didn't?' She stared at him. 'But I...' Then the penny dropped and she smiled. 'Ask me again. Properly.'

He stood up and pulled her to her feet, then dropped to one knee in front of her. 'Take the sunrise as read. We're on a cliff overlooking the sea and it's a bright new day ahead.' He smiled. 'Melinda Fortesque, I love you. Will you do me the honour of becoming my wife?'

'Yes. Yes, please.'

He whooped, stood up, then picked her up and spun her

round. And then kissed her, hot and sweet and slow. Telling her with his body as well as his mouth that he loved her. 'I did this all the wrong way round. I should've bought you a ring.' He dropped a kiss on the ring finger of her left hand.

'It doesn't matter. We can choose one together.' She blinked back the tears. 'Dragan. You really want to marry me?'

He nodded. 'Though I really should have asked your father for his permission first.'

Her father. Oh, lord. How could she tell Dragan that he'd have to ask the king of Contarini for his permission?

And would he even want to ask her father once she told him who she was? That thing he'd said about being a better man…Would knowing the truth about her background make him want to walk away?

This was getting messier and messier. She didn't want to lose the man she loved. She couldn't keep lying to him, but how could she tell him the truth? 'No need,' she said quickly.

He frowned slightly, and she flinched inwardly. How tactless could she get? He'd just told her that he'd lost his family—and it would sound to him as if she was dismissing hers. Which she wasn't… But her family came with complications. *Major* complications. 'It's the twenty-first century and I'm a modern woman,' she said softly. 'I can make my own decisions. And I choose to accept your proposal.' She stroked his face. 'I would be honoured to be your wife, Dragan.'

'Then we'll talk to Reverend Kenner,' he said. 'Unless you'd prefer something less traditional?'

'No. I'd like nothing more than to marry you at St Mark's.' The beautiful little parish church with its lych-gate—so different from her own parish church and all that heavy, overpowering gilding. Tourists loved her family church in Contarini, whereas Melinda had always found it oppressive.

She much preferred small, quiet, simple English country churches like the one here in Penhally. 'With all the spring blossom around. Like confetti falling on us—but we can't have confetti.'

'Why not?'

'Because foil isn't biodegradable and it can choke birds, and the paper sort contains dyes and bleach.'

He smiled. 'Trust you to know that sort of thing.'

'I'm a vet. Of *course* I know that sort of thing.' She thought for a moment. 'Dried flower petals are fine. Or the stuff that contains seeds for the birds.'

'Whatever you want, *carissima*. So when do you want to get married? Summer?'

'Spring,' she said, stroking his face. '*This* spring. Because I can't wait to be your wife.' She reached up to kiss him. 'I love you, Dragan. I really, really love you. I hope you know that.'

'I do. And I love you, too.' He held her close. 'But I do need to buy you a proper ring. I was going to suggest going shopping this weekend, but I'm doing Saturday morning surgery.'

'Me, too—but I'm not on call in the afternoon. Are you?'

'No. OK, we'll go and choose a ring together then. And move your stuff across from the flat to here. If you want to, that is,' he added diffidently.

'Of *course* I want to.'

He smiled. 'I never knew life could be so perfect.'

'Me, too.' There was a definite stormcloud ahead, in the shape of her family—but then again, they'd had to accept that she had the right to choose her job. They'd have to accept that she had the right to choose her own life partner, too. That she'd chosen the man she loved—and that he loved her right back.

As long as Dragan knew she loved him, that who she was really didn't matter, everything was going to be just fine.

She'd find the right words to explain.

Soon.

CHAPTER THREE

DRAGAN'S estate car wasn't parked outside the little terraced cottage. It didn't necessarily mean the doctor was out, Nick thought. It might be that he hadn't been able to find a parking space on Harbour Road. Although it wasn't yet peak season, the tourists had already started to trickle into the village.

Nick rapped on the door and waited.

No reply.

So obviously Dragan was either still out on house calls or he'd gone somewhere—probably with Melinda, if the village gossip was correct. The Croatian doctor was always so close-mouthed—in over two years of working together at the practice, Nick still really didn't know him that well. Dragan wasn't one to sit in the staffroom and chat over coffee and Cornish fairings with the rest of the team. He was brilliant at his job, and the staff at the practice adored him because he was always even-tempered and polite and remembered everyone's birthdays, but as to what made the man tick…It was anybody's guess.

Nick shrugged, resigned. Never mind. He could catch Dragan tomorrow morning before surgery.

And then the front door of the cottage next door opened.

'Well, hel-*lo*,' a voice drawled.

Nick looked across at the woman leaning against the door.

Her jeans did nothing to disguise her curves—or just how long her legs were. Her green eyes held the most sexy come-hither look he'd ever seen. And her long blonde hair was slightly tousled, as if she'd just got out of bed—despite the fact that it was late afternoon.

His body tightened at the thought.

'I'm Natasha Wakefield,' she said.

'Nick Tremayne.' He smiled at her. 'Are you new to the village?'

She shrugged. 'Maybe, maybe not. I'll see how it goes. It was time for a change of scene.'

A woman with complications, then. So maybe he'd better squash the impulse to ask her out to dinner. Complications were the last thing he needed. In his eyes nowadays it was fun or nothing. So he brought the subject back to what he really wanted to know. 'Do you know if Dragan is in?'

'Dragan?' she asked, mystified.

Clearly—despite living next door to her—Dragan hadn't introduced himself. Which didn't surprise Nick in the slightest: Dragan really guarded his privacy. 'The man who lives here,' Nick explained.

'Oh, *him*.' She waved a dismissive hand. 'He's off somewhere with Blondie and Hopalong.'

It took Nick a moment to realise that Natasha meant Melinda and Bramble. And although he didn't like the idea of anyone making fun of the quiet, serious doctor he'd come to rely on more and more since Marco had gone back to Italy, he acknowledged the aptness of her remark. Melinda's hair was striking, and the dog was still limping slightly despite the pins and plate that held her broken leg. 'Never mind, I'll catch him at the surgery tomorrow.'

'You're a doctor?' She looked surprised. 'You don't look like one.'

He knew she was angling but he couldn't resist it—this

might be fun. And he could do with some fun in his life right now. 'What do I look like?'

'The kind of man who sails fast boats.'

He laughed. 'I haven't done that for a long time.'

'Maybe,' she said, 'you ought to. I know someone with a boat. Come out with me tomorrow.'

Her mouth was incredibly sensual. If they weren't so short-staffed at the practice, he could've been tempted. Seriously tempted. 'Sorry, I'm on duty.'

'Ah. The kind of dedicated doctor who won't play hookey.'

'Is that such a bad thing?' he asked mildly.

'Maybe not.' She looked at him through lowered eyelashes, and he noticed again what an intense green her eyes were. 'But if you work hard, you need to play hard to balance it out.'

A definite offer. And if there were no strings—why not? 'Have dinner with me tonight, then.'

'That,' she said, 'might be…interesting.'

Nick felt his libido stir. A pub meal at the Penhally Arms would hardly be to the tastes of a woman like Natasha. 'There's a nice little restaurant in Rock.'

She wrinkled her nose. His surprise must have shown on his face because she added, 'I'm from Rock. I eat there all the time. *Bor*-ing. How about somewhere different—somewhere local?'

The Anchor Hotel, then: the most upmarket that Penhally had to offer. 'Sure. I'll pick you up at…' he glanced at his watch '…seven.'

She smiled. 'It's a date.'

Melinda's mobile phone rang. She made an apologetic face at Dragan as she answered it. 'I'm on call. Sorry,' she mouthed.

'It's fine. I know what it's like,' he reassured her quietly.

'Melinda? Oh, thank God. It's Violet Kennedy. I'm sorry to bother you, but it's my Cassidy. He's not at all well.'

Even though the parrot was the elderly widow's closest companion, Melinda knew that Violet wasn't one to panic. For her to call out of hours, the parrot must really be ill.

'Try not to worry,' she said quietly. 'I'll come out to see him. Now, if you tell me his symptoms, if I'm not sure what's wrong I can talk to one of my former colleagues, who's a specialist in birds, and he'll give us advice.'

She took a notepad from her handbag and scribbled down the list of symptoms. 'I'll be with you very soon, I promise.' She ended the call, then turned to Dragan, who had pulled into a layby. 'Sorry, I don't think we'll be having dinner out after all. Do you want to drop me back at the surgery?'

'You don't have the same patient confidentiality rules that I do—I'll come with you, if you like,' he suggested.

She smiled. 'You'll be my assistant?'

'Well, I can drive you while you're talking to your colleague. Do you need me to take you back to the surgery for your contact book?'

She waved her phone at him 'It's all here. But you are an angel. Do you know Violet Kennedy?'

'She's one of my patients, actually—so, yes. And I know the quickest way to get to her house from here.'

'*Bene.*' She leaned over and kissed him. 'You will be the perfect vet's husband.'

He smiled. 'And you'll be the perfect doctor's wife.'

Dragan turned the car round and drove them back to Penhally as Melinda rang her former colleague. 'Hello, Jake? It's Melinda Fortesque. How are you?'

'Fine. Long time, no hear.'

'I know. I'm terrible. Listen, Jake, I'm sorry to bother you, especially out of hours, but this is your field and I need a specialist in exotics.'

Jake gave a resigned sigh. 'Hit me with it, then.'

'African grey parrot, we think about forty years old. He's

being sick and has diarrhoea—and I think his owner's panick-
ing a bit about bird flu.'

Although Dragan wasn't consciously listening in and he
was concentrating on driving, he couldn't help overhearing
the conversation. And Melinda was just as he'd expected her
to be with her colleague—warm, friendly, open—and her
answers were concise and thorough. No longwindedness.

'No, it's just him and his owner,' Melinda said. 'No, just
his normal diet—bird seed, apples, bananas and sweetcorn.'
She paused. 'Yes, I have some at the surgery. Crop needle?
Oh…' She grimaced. 'Yes, you did teach me. OK. Yes. I'll
do that. Thank you.' Another pause. 'Are you sure?' She
smiled. 'You are a wonderful man. I will make you my chocolate and hazelnut torte. Really, I will. Thank you.' She ended
the call. 'Dragan, can we go back to the surgery so I can pick
up some powders and some equipment?'

'Of course.'

'Jake was the head of my old practice in Exeter. He spe-
cialised in exotics—there's nothing he doesn't know about
parrots. He thinks the bird's probably eaten something when
his owner wasn't looking.'

'So what are the powders you were talking about?'

'Electrolyte replacement.'

'The same sort of thing I'd give a child with sickness and
diarrhoea to stop dehydration,' Dragan said thoughtfully.
'Except the dose would be different.'

She nodded. 'It's good stuff—it helps to flush the kidneys
into proper working order again.'

When they'd collected the equipment, he drove them out
to Violet Kennedy's towards the edge of the village.

Violet opened the door, her face lined with worry. 'Thank
you so much for coming, Melinda.'

'That's what I'm here for. I have an assistant with me,' she
said with a smile. 'I believe you know him.'

Despite her obvious worry, Violet smiled at him. 'Dr Lovak, how nice to see you.'

'And you, Mrs Kennedy.'

The parrot, which was usually strutting on its perch, showing off its glorious black and crimson tail feathers or throwing a toy around, and which greeted all visitors with a piercing whistle and ''Ow do, m'dear?' before shocking them with a barrage of ripe language, was hunched in the corner of the cage, absolutely silent. Dragan cast a worried look at Melinda. If the bird died, he really wasn't sure that Violet Kennedy would be able to cope. Since her husband's death, she'd lavished most of her love on the parrot; her children and grandchildren lived in London, so she didn't see anywhere near as much of them as she'd like.

'Oh, Cassidy, *tesoro*, what have you done to yourself?' Melinda crooned, and rubbed his poll. She gently lifted him out of the cage and felt his feet. 'Violet, do you have a hot-water bottle, please? I need to keep him warm and that's the best thing. I need some hot water, too, please. And two small cups, a bowl and a spoon, if I may?'

Violet looked grim. 'I'll put the kettle on. So do you think it's bird flu?'

'No, I don't,' Melinda reassured her. 'There haven't been any reports of dead wild birds in the area, there are no problems at the local poultry farms, and to be honest he's an indoor bird, not kept outside in an aviary—so even if there were problems outside he'd be at very, very low risk.'

'So what's wrong?' Dragan asked, keeping his voice low.

'His feet are cold. That's not good. I'll need to start treatment for the dehydration now, but Jake said if his feet are cold I'll be better off looking after him at the surgery in a heated cage.' She bit her lip. 'Violet really isn't going to like this.'

'She'll understand if it's best for Cassidy.'

Violet returned with a hot-water bottle. 'Where do you want the other things?'

'In the kitchen, please. I need to mix up some powders—they'll help replace the salt and sugar in his blood and make him feel better.' She paused. 'Has Cassidy eaten anything other than his normal diet? Could he have, I don't know, taken something from your plate while you answered the phone or something?'

'I don't think so.' Violet looked thoughtful. 'The grandchildren were visiting until yesterday and they had one Easter egg I'd given them.'

'And they fed some chocolate to the bird as a treat?'

Violet shook her head. 'I don't think they would. And they know I keep chocolate in the drawer, but…no, they wouldn't have done that.'

'Can Cassidy open drawers with his beak?' Melinda asked.

Violet was silent for a moment, her brow crumpled. 'He's a clever old bird. Maybe.' She pulled open one of the dresser drawers. 'Oh! The children wouldn't have ripped open a packet of chocolate buttons and left them like that. They're little monkeys but they're not bad kids.' She shook her head. 'Well, I never. He must have opened the packet, eaten some, and closed the drawer again.'

'As you say, he's a clever bird,' Melinda said. 'And chocolate buttons could well be what's making him feel so ill now. One thing my colleague told me, parrots can't eat avocados or chocolate. They're both poisonous for parrots.'

'Poisonous?'

She nodded. 'It doesn't take much—only fifty grams of chocolate, just one small packet of buttons, could be fatal. So I'd keep them locked away in future, if I were you, or in an airtight container you know for sure he can't open.'

Violet went pale. 'Is he going to die?'

'Not if I can help it. Because I promised to teach him Italian—did I not, *tesoro*?' She rubbed the bird's poll again. 'Come on. Let's get you feeling better.' She smiled at Dragan. 'I wasn't joking about you being my assistant, by the way.'

He spread his hands. 'Just tell me what to do.'

'OK. We're going to make up some powders for Cassidy, and I'm going to feed him through a crop needle and a syringe so I can make sure he gets enough.'

'A bit like when babies are too sick to eat and they need feeding by a tube,' Dragan added, seeing the worry on Violet's face. 'It's a very common procedure and it doesn't hurt.'

'*Essatamente*,' Melinda said. 'And just to make sure—do you have any olive oil, Violet?'

'I've got sunflower oil,' Violet said.

'That will do nicely. I need to put it on the needle—he's dehydrated and his throat will be dry, so the oil will lubricate the needle and make sure it doesn't hurt him.' She nodded to the bowls on the table. 'Dragan, can you put the hot water in the bowl for me? And, Violet, I need you to cuddle Cassidy with the hot-water bottle. *Bene*, just like that.'

Dragan noticed how she involved Violet and talked her through the treatment without being patronising. She would've made a fabulous doctor for human patients too, he thought.

She was gentle with the bird, but even so when she'd finished the old lady was clearly only just holding back tears. 'My Cassidy. What will I do without you?' she whispered.

'I want to take him back to the surgery with me,' Melinda said gently. 'It will take him a few days to get over this. He needs to be in a heated cage so he doesn't get cold, and we'll need to feed him this mixture twice a day until he's able to eat normal food again. And then I'll bring him home safely to you, I promise.'

'Cassidy's been with me for years,' Violet said. 'My husband got him for me when he was in the navy. I…I can't imagine not having him.'

'I'll bring him home to you as soon as I can,' Melinda re-assured her, 'and you can visit any time you like.' She rubbed the bird's poll. 'We'll have you back with your *mamma* soon.

And while you're at the surgery I can teach you some words of love in Italian—then you can charm people instead of swearing like a sailor and making your *mamma* turn red every time the vicar calls round, yes?'

The bird—which Dragan knew from experience would usually tell her where to go in extremely colourful language—made no response.

And he could see just how worried Violet looked. He squeezed her hand. 'Try not to worry. Melinda knows what she's doing.'

'I know you'll do your best,' Violet said, her voice slightly shaky.

'Normally I'd suggest transporting him in a cage,' Melinda said, 'but as he's so ill and so cold, he's not going to move around much. He can sit and have a cuddle on my lap on the way to the surgery, if you don't mind lending me that hot-water bottle until tomorrow. And Dragan will drive us very, very carefully. I'll call you when we're back at the surgery so you won't have to worry. And I'll call you tomorrow morning to let you know how he's doing.'

Exactly the same kind of care and reassurance that he gave his own patients, Dragan thought. And he could've hugged her for it. Just as Lizzie had said the previous day, Melinda was a gem. She recognised that the family had needs as well as the patient.

He drove them back to the surgery, and followed Melinda inside. She sorted out a heated cage and made the parrot comfortable, then called Jake for a quick confab about the treatment plan.

'It always surprises me how small your theatres are compared to ours,' Dragan remarked when she'd finished.

Melinda smiled. 'My patients are usually a lot smaller than yours. I don't really need a seven-foot-long table for a Jack Russell.'

'No, I suppose not.'

'Poor Cassidy. I never thought I'd see the day when this bird was quiet,' Melinda said, looking at the parrot. 'I really want to keep an eye on him for a while.'

'Do you want to stay here tonight?' he asked. With her flat being just above the surgery, it made sense.

'If you don't mind sharing a single bed.'

'Now, I'm the one who's meant to be Spartan,' he teased. 'Of course I don't mind. I'll go and get us some fish and chips, shall I, while you call Violet and let her know how Cassidy has settled in?'

She kissed him. 'Most men would not be this understanding, Dragan. You are...' she smiled '...*meraviglioso*.'

'Tell me that when I'm on call and the phone goes at two a.m. and I have to go out to a patient,' he said dryly.

'That, I won't mind. But then you'll come back and warm your feet on me.'

'When you're all warm and soft and irresistible.' Dragan kissed her. 'I'll be back in ten minutes, *piccola*.'

Melinda had just finished reassuring Violet when her mobile phone rang. She glanced at the screen and grimaced. Her mother. Please, don't let this be another call about duty and how she really ought to stop playing at being a country vet and come home. Because it wasn't going to happen: she was staying right here where she belonged. Melinda Lovak, country vet and doctor's wife.

Which was something else she needed to tell her parents. Though she'd need to choose her words very carefully—which meant maybe not tonight. If she made the call rather than took it, she'd feel more in control and not so much on the defensive.

She pressed the answer button. '*Buona sera, Mamma*.'

'*Buona sera*, Melinda. I am sorry to call you so late. But I have some bad news.'

CHAPTER FOUR

MELINDA went cold. '*Papà*?'

'No, he is fine.' Her mother sighed. 'It's Raffi.'

Here we go again, Melinda thought. Her older brother Raphael had done something stupid and she was expected to come to the rescue—because it seemed she was the only one who could ever get through to him. Raffi ignored whatever Serena said because she was the baby; though most of the time he didn't listen to Melinda either. 'What is it this time? He was caught *in flagrante delicto* with someone and she's sold her story to the press? He's in debt at Monte Carlo? He raced his new boat against someone and lost it in a bet?' Raphael had done all three over the last two years, and he never seemed to learn from his mistakes. Sometimes Melinda thought he actually *enjoyed* repeating them. He'd talked about sailing over to see her, but she'd been quick to give him the impression that Penhally was a complete backwater and he'd be bored, bored, bored within two seconds—the last thing she wanted was for him to cut a swathe through the female population of Penhally and leave her to pick up the pieces afterwards.

'No.'

There was a pause in which Melinda thought she detected a sob—then again, Viviana Fortesque would never lose that much control. Melinda must've imagined it.

'He's dead.'

Dead? The word seemed to be coming from the far end of a long, long tunnel. She couldn't take it in. Raffi, her brother who was much larger than life and more than lived every minute to the full, dead? 'No. There must be some mistake. He can't be.'

'He died yesterday afternoon.'

'What?' She dragged in a breath. 'What happened?'

'He was driving.'

Too fast, the way Raffi always did. She didn't need to be told that. Even losing his licence for three months hadn't stopped him speeding the second he'd got his licence back.

'He spun off the road and hit a tree.'

'Oh, *Dio.* Was anyone else hurt?'

'He was on his own in the car.'

Which was a good thing, in one sense: at least no other family was going to have to go through this aching loss, this misery at losing a loved one too soon. But all the same, her heart ached for him. There had been nobody to hold his hand at the end, nobody to tell him they loved him. And even though he'd been a selfish, spoiled brat and sometimes she'd wanted to throttle him, nobody deserved an end like that. 'Poor Raffi. So he died all alone,' she said softly.

'No, your father and I were with him at the end.'

'But…' Melinda frowned, not understanding. 'You said he was alone in the car.'

'He was.' Viviana's voice was dry. 'It's been touch and go for the last couple of days whether he would pull through.'

It took a moment to sink in. And when it did, Melinda was furious. 'Hang on, it happened a couple of days ago? My brother was in hospital—in Intensive Care—and you didn't call me?'

'There was no point. You wouldn't have come.'

Oh, this was outrageous. Not only had her family kept the

news of Raffi's accident from her, now they were trying to make her feel guilty about it. Thinking for her instead of letting her make her own decisions. Just the way it had always been.

And they'd taken away her chance to say goodbye.

She'd never forgive them for this.

And how come she hadn't read about in the papers? Unless her parents had hushed it up. Come to some agreement with the press so Raffi wouldn't be hounded in hospital by the paparazzi.

'Of course I would have come,' she said through gritted teeth. 'He's my brother.'

'Apart from the fact you two barely speak when you do see each other,' Viviana pointed out, 'you're still playing at being an English country vet.'

'I am *not* playing.' She twisted the end of her hair round her fingers. 'This is my life now, Mamma, my career, and—' The twisted hair started to hurt, and the pain brought her back to her senses. What was she doing, letting her mother get to her like this? 'I am not going to argue with you. Not with Raffi dead. It's the wrong time.' And surely even her mother would see that. 'When is the funeral?' She just about managed to bite back, *Or weren't you going to tell me about that either?*

'Two days' time.'

'Then I will come back to Contarini.'

'*Bene.* I will send the jet tonight to your nearest airport. Which is…?'

'I can't fly out tonight. *Mamma*, I have responsibilities here.'

'You have responsibilities to your family, Melinda,' Viviana said, her voice like cut glass.

'I can't just drop everything and leave George to sort out my patients and my surgery tomorrow. It's not fair. We need time to sort out a locum for me.'

'Locum?' There was a shocked pause. 'You mean, you are actually planning to go back again?'

'Of course. It's my job. My vocation, *Mamma*.' Not to mention the fact the man she loved and was going to marry lived here in Cornwall. Though now was most definitely not the time to tell her mother about that.

'While you were the middle child, we were prepared to let you play.'

Play? A degree in veterinary sciences meant long hours and hard work. Years and years of study and exams. She twisted her hair again, and the sharp pain made her pause instead of saying something she knew she'd regret. She'd let that 'play' comment slide. For now. 'Nothing has changed.'

'Raffi is dead. You are the eldest now. Which means that you have responsibilities and duties here, Melinda. You are the next in line to the throne, and you need to come back to Contarini for good.'

'I'll come back for Raffi's funeral and to see you, *Papà* and Serena. But I'm not promising any more than that.'

'Why must you be so difficult? So headstrong?' Viviana demanded.

Headstrong? Melinda nearly laughed. She wasn't the one who drove fast cars and fast boats and fast planes, who went through money as if a fresh supply could be printed every day, or whose champagne bill was legendary. She was the one who'd always been quiet, bookish, who'd spent her time in the stables and the kennels. Raffi was the headstrong one and Serena was the one who wore pretty dresses and had beautiful manners and charmed people. Melinda was the odd one out, and everyone knew it. A very square peg whose corners just couldn't be rubbed off to make her fit the role they wanted her to take.

A role she didn't want.

A role she'd *never* wanted.

'*Mamma*, I am too tired to argue. I can't fly out tonight. I'll talk to George, then I'll catch a flight from here to London tomorrow and from London to…' She thought rapidly. Palermo was nearer to Contarini, but Naples was probably a little more discreet. 'To Napoli. I'll text you to let you know my flight times, *d'accordo*?'

'Then we will see you tomorrow.'

And that was it. The line went dead. No 'I love you'. No warmth or affection. Just as it had always been when she had been growing up—her parents had always been too busy and their duty had come first.

Maybe, she thought, if Viviana and Alessandro Fortesque had spent more time with their children, Raffi would have learned to control his impulses.

Gritting her teeth, she dialled her boss's number. She knew the burly vet would be understanding, but she still hated the fact that she was letting him down.

'George? I'm sorry to bother you on your night off.' She took a deep breath. 'My mother just called. I need to go home for a few days.'

'Something's wrong?'

'My brother…died. In a car crash.' It felt weird, saying it. And she felt cold, so cold. She really needed Dragan. Needed to feel his arms round her.

'Oh, love, I'm so sorry. Of course you have to go. Look, I can cover for you tonight. Go now. Don't worry about a thing.'

Dear George. She could have hugged him. 'I can't get a flight until tomorrow anyway. I'll still do tonight on call. But if I could leave first thing in the morning—and I'll write down a list of my patients and what have you—that'd be…' She swallowed hard. 'That'd be really appreciated.'

'Are you on your own? Do you want me to come over, or do you want to come over to us?'

George, his wife and four children lived in a sprawling old farmhouse just outside Penhally. At the Smiths', you could always be sure of a warm welcome, a cat to curl on your lap in the big farmhouse kitchen and a dog to sit by your feet.

'No, no. I'll be fine. I'm, um…Dragan is keeping me company this evening. I'm hoping I don't get another callout because I have Cassidy here.'

'Violet's parrot? Why?'

'I think he ate some chocolate and his system's reacting to it.'

'Chocolate's poisonous to parrots—as well as to dogs,' George said.

'*Essatamente*. So he needs nursing here in a heated cage for a few days. I've given him the electrolyte powders tonight, but he'll need them twice a day and a gradual return to his normal diet.'

'Leave me your treatment plan and I'll ask Sally to come in early tomorrow and take over,' George said.

Melinda was happy that the practice nurse would follow the treatment plan exactly. And she was so experienced that she'd probably seen a few sick parrots in her time: Melinda often thought Sally knew as much as the vets did. 'George, thank you so much. I really hate it that I'm letting you down. And if I'm not back by Saturday—'

'Then young Tina Chamberlain can shadow *me* for the morning. She might like to come and see what we do with the livestock, so she sees the other side of the practice and not just the small-animal work,' George finished. 'I'll clear it with Lizzie first. Don't worry about a thing. Just ring me if you need me or there's anything I can do, all right? And we'll see you when we see you.'

'Thank you, George.'

She'd just put the phone down when the doorbell rang. Dragan.

She went down to meet him and unlock the door; he followed her back up the stairs to her small kitchen, carrying two wrapped parcels. 'Sorry I was so long. There was a queue, and then I had to wait for fresh chips. But at least they're really hot,' he said with a smile. And then he frowned, taking in her expression. 'What's wrong, Melinda? Cassidy's worse?'

'No.' She dragged in a breath. 'My mother called. My brother…' She rubbed a hand over her face. She still couldn't quite believe it. 'He died yesterday after a car accident.'

'Oh, Melinda.' He put the fish and chips on the worktop and held her close. 'I'm so sorry.'

'I have to go back.'

'Of course you do. How are you getting there?'

'I haven't booked a flight yet. But I'll take the first one I can get tomorrow from Newquay to Gatwick, and then Gatwick to Naples.'

Dragan could remember the feeling. The black hole inside when he realised he'd lost his entire family. That he was the only one left. And although he realised that Melinda wasn't close to her own family, he knew she would do the right thing. She'd go back and help her family with the funeral, comfort her parents.

Though it was a tough thing to do on your own. Especially when you felt you didn't fit in—the one thing she *had* admitted to him over the last few months.

'Do you want me to come with you?' he asked, stroking her hair. 'For support?'

'Bless you for asking, but no. I can do this.'

But her expression was grim. She was clearly dreading this. 'Melinda, you're not on your own,' he said softly. 'You have me. And if there's anything I can do, all you have to do is say so.'

'Right now, just hold me. Please.' Her voice sounded hoarse, broken—as if she was trying to hold back her tears. Typical Melinda, being brave and not leaning on anyone else.

'Let the tears come, *piccola*,' he said softly. 'They will help.'

She dragged in a breath. 'Right now I feel like the most selfish, horrible woman in the world.'

'Why?' He really didn't follow. Ignoring the fish and chips, he led her over to the sofa and settled her on his lap.

'Because you…you've lost your family. And you were close to them. I'm not close to mine—and I feel horrible telling you that, because I have what you've lost and I don't want you to think I'm just…oh…not appreciating it, throwing it all away like a toddler having a tantrum with her toys.'

'Of course I don't. I'd already guessed you weren't close to them. But it doesn't make me love you any less. Not all families are like mine—I see plenty of difficult relationships in my job,' he reminded her. 'Let me go with you, *tesoro*. So at least you have someone on your side.'

For a moment he thought she was going to say yes. But then she shook her head. 'I won't drag you into all this mess. And I…I could strangle Raffi for being so reckless, so stupid. And my parents, for not letting me say goodbye to him. The accident happened days ago. He died yesterday. And they didn't tell me until *today*, until after he was dead and it was too late for me to say goodbye.'

'Maybe it was grief,' he suggested. 'Maybe they couldn't find the words to tell you.' It had been hard for him to tell people after his family had been wiped out. Most of the time it had hurt too much to articulate. And when he had managed to say it, the pity on other people's faces had choked him.

'It's not just them. I'm so angry with him.'

Anger was one of the stages of grief, he knew, along with denial and bargaining and depression. And finally there would be acceptance. But she really needed to talk about this. As she'd said to him so recently, bottling things up made them worse. 'Why?' he asked softly.

'He always had to have the fastest car. And he always drove like a maniac. He knew *Papà* was expecting him to take over—but would he be careful? No. Scrape after scrape after scrape. And I always had to bail him out.' She shook her head. 'The day before my Finals started, he expected me to go back to Contarini and sort things out with our parents. He'd been stupid and lost a lot of money in a card game.'

So her parents were wealthy? Dragan wasn't that surprised. She had an air of breeding about her. Though he'd just bet she'd been like him and worked her own way through college—not because she'd had to but because she was too independent to rely on a silver spoon.

Maybe that was why she'd reacted so badly to his teasing 'princessy' comment.

'But I said no. I'd worked too hard for my exams to give it all up for something I knew would just happen again and again—because Raffi only ever did what he wanted and he never stopped to think things through before he acted.' She gritted her teeth. 'And he barely spoke to me afterwards, because I made him stand on his own two feet for once.'

'He probably still knew you loved him.'

'And that's another reason I don't like myself. Because I'm not so sure I *did* love him.'

'You can love someone without liking them,' Dragan pointed out, stroking her hair.

'I don't fit in with my family. I never have. And I know the second I step off that plane the pressure's going to start.'

'Pressure?'

'To go back to Contarini. To do what they want me to do. Give up being a vet—but I can't. This is who I *am,* Dragan.'

'Then let me come with you. Take some of the flak for you.'

'You can't.' She shook her head. 'That's really not fair to you.'

'*Carissima*, you didn't ask. I offered. Look, I've lived

through a war. Nothing scares me any more because I know there is always a light at the end of the tunnel, no matter how dark things seem at the time. And I can help you through this.'

'You *can't,*' she repeated. 'We've got that appointment lined up with Reverend Kenner tomorrow.'

'He won't mind putting it back. Besides, I can't discuss the wedding without you.'

'Yes, you can. Otherwise it holds everything up.'

He frowned. 'What difference does a couple of days make? Why the hurry?'

'Because I don't want to wait for the rest of my life to start.'

Something was going on here, and he really wasn't sure what it was.

'Dragan. I love you,' she said softly. Urgently. 'I want to marry you and I don't want my family interfering.'

He didn't understand why they'd interfere. At twenty-seven, Melinda was more than capable of making her own choices. 'So you haven't told them yet? About us, I mean?'

She shook her head. 'And now isn't the right time. Not with Raffi's funeral.'

'But if you want to get married as soon as we can, you'll have to give them some notice. Surely they'll want to come to the wedding?'

'I'll tell them when we've set a date. Which you and Reverend Kenner can sort out tomorrow.' She twisted her hair round her fingers. 'At least I'll be able to come home to you and to happy news.'

He rested his cheek against her hair. 'All right. If that's really what you want me to do. But at least let me drive you to the airport tomorrow. And I can pick you up when you get back.'

'Thank you.' She held him tightly, almost as if she were drowning and he was the only thing keeping her afloat. 'Dragan. There is something I should tell you about, something we need to discuss. Something…'

She sounded worried sick, and he dropped a kiss on her forehead. 'Not now. You've just had a horrible shock. Whatever it is, it can wait until you're back from Contarini. Everything's going to be fine.'

'I love you. And I don't deserve you.'

He scoffed. 'Of course you do.' Or was this why she wasn't close to her family? Was this why she'd chosen to move to another country, because they were always putting her down and telling her she wasn't good enough? Wealthy parents were often ambitious for their children—and if she'd resisted going into a long-standing family business, that was probably the root of the difficulties between them. A career that would make any other parents proud might disappoint hers because they'd expected something else for her. 'And I love you, too. You need to book that flight—but eat first.'

She grimaced. 'I can't face anything. Not now.'

'And the chips are probably cold by now. I could put them in the microwave,' he suggested.

'Dragan Lovak, and you a doctor!' She shook her head in apparent disbelief. 'Tut-tut. Think of the bacteria. Reheated food that hasn't been chilled properly in between...it's an absolute breeding ground. And, besides, the chips will go soggy if you put them in the microwave.'

'Perhaps you're right.' But at least he'd made her smile again.

Though the look in her eyes disturbed him. The desperation. Would it really be so bad for her, going back? 'I'm here,' he said softly. 'And nothing's going to hurt you while I'm around.'

If only that were true. As soon as he found out about her family...Oh, *Dio*. She had to tell him, she really did. But now wasn't the time or the place. And he'd said it could wait...

Coward that she was, she was relieved. The risk of losing

the man she loved right on top of losing her brother was just too horrible to contemplate. She knew he'd be hurt that she hadn't told him before—and maybe angry that she hadn't trusted him—and she felt bad about it. Guilty. But she just hadn't been able to find the right words or the right time.

Though she'd tell him the truth about herself tomorrow morning. First thing.

CHAPTER FIVE

'I'LL go and check on Bramble,' Dragan said, 'while you sort out your flights.'

'You can bring her back here, if you like,' Melinda said. 'She's no trouble.'

Having a dog to make a fuss of might help her, he thought.

Even though he lived just round the corner, to save time in the morning he drove over to Melinda's and left his car in the surgery car park. If people talked—well, let them. After his meeting with Reverend Kenner tomorrow, everyone would know anyway.

Melinda had given him her key; he unlocked the door to her flat and carried Bramble up the stairs. Strictly speaking, he knew she could manage it herself, but he also knew what a lively dog she was—and her leg still hadn't healed properly. If she slipped on the stairs and cracked a bone or shifted the pins again, she might have to lose the leg. And he really wanted to avoid that if possible.

The dog took full advantage of her position to lick his face, and he laughed. 'You horrible mutt. What are you? Horrible!'

She licked him again, clearly hearing in his tone of voice how much he loved her. She reminded him of the dog he'd had as a boy. So when Melinda had been looking for a home for the dog she'd rescued, a few months before, he hadn't been able to resist offering.

'How did you get on?' he asked Melinda as he set the dog back on her feet.

'I've done some notes for George and Sally, and there's a flight to London at twenty past seven tomorrow morning. I can pick up my tickets from the desk, but I need to be at the airport an hour before my flight.'

'Crack of dawn start, then.' He shrugged. 'Not a problem. I'll just go and fetch my clothes and Bramble's basket from the car.'

When he returned, Bramble was settled very comfortably, thank you, on the sofa, and Melinda was making a fuss of her.

'Don't think you're sleeping there tonight, dog,' he warned.

Bramble just thumped her tail, as if she knew perfectly well that Melinda wouldn't mind.

'I'll make us something to eat,' Dragan said. 'And, no, Bramble, you are not scoffing all the cold, soggy chips,' he added at the dog's hopeful look when he carried the paper parcel over to the bin. 'They're bad for you.'

'Don't do anything for me. I'm really not hungry,' Melinda said with a grimace.

'You need to eat,' he said gently. 'Trust me, low blood sugar on top of the bad news you've just had will only make you feel worse. Now, you go and check on Cassidy, and I'll make you an omelette.' At her raised eyebrow, he smiled. 'I make a very good omelette, I'll have you know.'

When she came back from checking on the parrot and the large, fluffy omelette was cooked, he divided it into two and slid it onto their plates.

She ate about three mouthfuls before pushing her plate away.

'It's that bad?' he asked.

'No, no.' She shook her head. 'I'm sorry. I just… It feels wrong to eat somehow. My brother's dead and here I am, stuffing my face. It's…*wrong*.'

'OK. I won't force you.' He scraped the contents of her plate into the bin and made short work of the washing-up. 'Come on. Let's try and get some sleep.' He looked at the dog, who was still curled happily on the sofa. 'Bramble, in your basket.'

'Oh, leave her,' Melinda said, her voice weary. 'It doesn't matter.'

He remembered that feeling, too. As if nothing mattered any more. And he ached for her.

'Come on, *cara*,' he said, and shepherded her into the bedroom. She used the little en suite bathroom first and by the time he'd had a quick shower and cleaned his teeth, she was curled up in bed.

'Have you set your alarm?' he asked.

She nodded.

'Good.' He slid his arm round her waist and drew her back into the curve of his body. Melinda was a bright, independent woman who was more than capable of standing on her own two feet—but tonight he felt very protective towards her. He wanted to be the barrier between her and the world, make sure nothing else happened to hurt her.

Clearly her family was nothing like his own had been. The trace of bitterness in her voice when she'd spoken about not fitting in…Well, she fitted in just fine with him. And together they'd make a new family. A family where she was the centre.

Ha. He hadn't even thought about children before. But now the idea had slid into his head, he liked it. And he could imagine their daughter—a small, stubborn version of Melinda, with his own dark eyes and hair and Melinda's beautiful smile. She'd wrap her daddy right round her little finger.

'*Volim te*,' he said softly, and kissed Melinda's bare shoulder.

He really hadn't intended to pressure her into making love with him. But when she twisted round in his arms, slid her arms round his neck and kissed him back, he couldn't help responding.

Her hand slid down over his shoulder, squeezed the firm muscles of his upper arms. 'You feel so good,' she whispered. And her mouth traced a path over his jawline, down his throat; her tongue pressed against the pulse point beating hard and fast in his neck.

'Ah, *bellissima*,' he muttered, and tipped his head back against the pillows, offering himself to her. If she wanted to take comfort from him, that was fine by him. He would tell her with his body that he was there for her, any time she needed him. That he loved her, wanted her, always would.

He dragged in a breath as she kissed her way down his breastbone. Her mouth was so soft, so sweet, and her hair felt like warm silk against his skin. He couldn't resist sliding his hands into the blonde tresses, urging her on. 'Melinda. You're driving me just a little bit crazy here.'

She lifted her head and her blue, blue eyes crinkled at the corners. 'Did you know, when you get turned on, your accent comes back a bit?'

'My accent?'

'Normally you sound very English. But when we make love…'

'I lose control,' he admitted.

'That's what I want. I want to make you feel the same way I feel.' She shifted to straddle him. He could feel the warmth of her sex against his erection and it made his pulse ratchet up that little bit more.

'I need to be inside you, Melinda,' he breathed.

'*Si*?' she teased, wriggling just enough to make him gasp.

In retaliation, he cupped her breasts, stroked the soft undersides and rubbed the pads of his thumbs against her nipples until she gave a sharp intake of breath.

'Dragan. I *need* you.'

He lifted his upper body from the bed so he could take first one and then the other nipple into his mouth, sucking hard. Her hands fisted in his hair and he could feel little shivers of desire running through her.

'Please, now,' she whispered. 'I need you now.'

'Let me get a condom.'

'No.' She leaned forward and kissed him hard. 'I don't want any barriers between us tonight.'

'Melinda, we should—' he began.

She pressed her forefinger lightly against his lips. 'It's OK. It's my safe time.'

The doctor in him knew there was no such thing as a safe time. Though he also knew exactly why she was asking him to do this: it was a way of fighting back against the spectre of death, of proving to herself that she was alive and kicking.

He shouldn't do this.

She was vulnerable.

And he was taking advantage of her. This had to stop.

'Tonight I need you close, Dragan.' She dragged in a breath. 'I want nothing between us. Just you and me.'

His heart overruled his head. How could he stop now, push her away and make her feel even worse? She needed comfort. She needed him. And if they made a baby tonight…then so be it. They were getting married in a few weeks in any case. He would've liked more time with her on his own, but if they made a child tonight he'd love their baby. Always. Just as he'd always love Melinda. She was the one who made him feel complete.

'I want you so badly,' she said, her voice hoarse. 'I need you. I love you. *Ti amo.*'

'I love you, too. Always. *Siempre.*'

She shifted slightly and slid her fingers around his erection, guided him to her entrance; he rocked his hips, easing inside her. Lord, she felt good, so warm and wet. Her eyes were almost black in the lamplight, her pupils dilated so he could barely see the iris. As turned on as he was. Needing this as much as he did. Right now they were as one—body, heart and soul.

And he never wanted this moment to end.

Her mouth opened in a soft sigh of pleasure as he began to move, a pleasure echoed in his own body as her muscles tightened round him and her movements mirrored his, lifting herself until he was almost out of her and then pushing down hard as he pushed up, taking him deeper than he could ever remember.

His fingers laced with hers and they gripped each other tightly as the tension ratcheted higher and higher.

'Dragan!' Her body started to ripple round his, and he could feel the tension in his own body reaching snapping point.

And then he was falling with her.

Over the edge, into a starburst.

She collapsed forwards onto him and he wrapped his arms round her; he could feel her heart beating rapidly against his chest, just as he knew she'd be able to feel the answering beat of his heart.

'I love you,' she whispered.

'I love you, too. And everything's going to be all right.'

'Is it?'

'Everything's going to be fine,' he promised her. 'Look, it's not too late to change your mind—I can maybe ask Lizzie Chamberlain to look after Bramble for me and come with you tomorrow.'

'No, I can't ask that of you—and you're short-staffed at the practice as it is.'

'They'll manage. We can get a locum. You're more important to me, *tesoro*. More important than anything else in the world.'

He could feel dampness against his chest and realised she was crying. Silently, with no shudders, as if she didn't have any strength to hold the tears back any more and they were just leaking out.

'Let it out, honey,' he whispered. 'Let the tears wash away the pain.'

She sobbed against him. 'I don't even know why I'm crying for him. Raffi was a selfish bastard and most of the time we didn't get on. He could be charming and good company—but most of the time he was a pain in the backside and he drove me demented with his thoughtlessness.'

'He was still your brother, still of your blood—there was still a bond between you, even when you fought.'

'I just don't want things to change between you and me. *Ever.*'

'Hey, why would they do that?' He lifted her slightly and kissed away her tears. 'I won't insist that you take my name, if you choose not to. Though I think it sounds nice. Melinda Lovak.' He kissed her gently. 'Beautiful. *Bellissima.* Like you.'

Her smile was wobbly, but at least it was a smile, he thought with relief. 'Of course I'll take your name, Dragan.'

'It's not a problem if you want to keep your maiden name for professional purposes.'

'No. But thank you for giving me the choice. For under-standing.'

Her words were heartfelt, he could tell—but he had no idea what she meant. Giving her the choice? But…why wouldn't she have a choice? This was the twenty-first century. He wouldn't expect her to give up her career. If they were blessed with children and she wanted to be a stay-at-home mum, that was fine; but if she wanted to combine a career and children, that was also fine. They'd work something out between them.

Maybe the root of this was in her relationship with her family. The fact they hadn't wanted her to be a vet—they'd wanted her to be part of the family firm, even though she was clearly born to be a vet. And she obviously felt guilty about the fact she had a family she wasn't close to, whereas he'd lost the ones he'd loved so much. Maybe when she came back from Contarini he'd persuade her to tell him about it. Get the bad memories out of her heart and replace them with happiness.

It took a while, but at last Dragan could tell from the regularity of Melinda's breathing that she'd fallen asleep. Though sleep eluded him. He was too worried about her.

He'd talk to Nick tomorrow morning, see if they could arrange a locum to cover him at the practice. Then he could go over to Contarini to give Melinda his support.

Then again, if her relationship with her family was that strained, this would be a seriously bad time to meet them. No way would her parents want to hear news of their daughter's wedding just before the funeral of their son.

Which left Dragan torn between being Melinda's support and abiding by her wishes: whatever he did, it didn't seem enough. For now all he could do was hold her while she slept. And when she came back to England he'd do his best to make her world a brighter place. Give her the happiness she deserved.

CHAPTER SIX

IT WAS still dark when Melinda's alarm beeped.

'Urgh. I am so not a morning person,' she grumbled. Especially today, knowing what she was going to face in Contarini.

And today, when she had to tell Dragan exactly what she was going back to. Why she was dreading it so much.

'I'll put the kettle on while you have a shower,' Dragan said.

By the time she'd dressed, he'd already made her a cup of coffee—strong and dark, just how she liked it—and he took a quick shower himself before he carried Bramble down the stairs to let her out. The dog, clearly sensing Melinda's need for comfort, insisted on sitting with her nose on Melinda's knee when Dragan brought her back up to the flat.

'All right, *cara*?' he asked.

No. Definitely not. But she tried to force a smile to her face. Be brave for him.

'Come on. You have to eat something.' He looked at the toast she'd crumbled onto her plate.

'I'm not hungry.' She felt too sick to eat. Sick with tension and guilt and misery and worry.

She had to tell him.

Now.

You're not just marrying the village vet. You're marrying…

'And we have to leave in ten minutes,' he warned her, after a quick glance at his watch.

'And I need to check on Cassidy before we go.' Which meant no time to talk. She couldn't neglect her professional duties. But she didn't want to neglect the love of her life either.

'Do you want me to hold him while you get the formula into him?'

She gave in. He was being so kind, so sweet—so caring. She couldn't tell him and expect him to cope with everything in the space of ten seconds before he helped her with her patient. 'Yes, please.'

They'd just finished when Sally walked in. Melinda gave the nurse the rundown on Cassidy's treatment plan and made sure she had Jake's number for queries.

And then it was time to go.

Dragan carried Bramble down to the car first, then brought Melinda's small flight bag and slid it onto the back seat. She locked the flat behind them and climbed into the car. Although she normally fiddled with his radio or the CD player, today she wanted silence. Silence to work out the right words to tell him. And Dragan was in tune with her mood enough not to push her to chatter.

She still hadn't worked out the right words by the time they got to the airport. Every time she tried to speak, it felt as if her tongue was glued to the roof of her mouth.

He left the window open enough to give Bramble some fresh air—he wouldn't be that long at the airport and, besides, it was still early morning and cool, so the car wouldn't become hot and uncomfortable for the dog.

'I'll carry this,' he said, hoisting Melinda's bag over his shoulder, and he walked hand in hand with her into the airport. He waited while she checked in at the reception desk and picked up her tickets, then walked with her to the departure lounge.

'Send me a text when you get there, so I know you've arrived safely,' he said, holding her close. 'I won't have my phone on during surgery, but I'll pick up your message as soon as I switch the phone on again.'

'OK. I'm not sure when I'll get a chance to ring you.' Her face was white. 'I really don't know what…' Her voice faded. Now. She had to tell him now.

Dragan, clearly oblivious to the real reason for her silence, squeezed her hand. 'Look, I'll call Nick. I'll sort out a locum and go back to Penhally to get someone to dog-sit Bramble and then I'll follow you straight out to Contarini. You don't have to face this on your own. I'll be there beside you.'

She swallowed hard, hating herself for being a liar and a fraud and hurting the man she loved. 'You are a good man, Dragan. I really don't deserve you.'

'Of course you do. Come with me and we'll sort out my tickets.'

'No, Dragan. I have to…' She dragged in a breath. 'I appreciate your offer, but I have to stand on my own two feet.'

'Sometimes,' he said with a sigh, 'I wish you weren't quite so independent. But I hope you know you can lean on me—that I'll never let you down.'

Oh, *Dio*. How could she do this? 'Dragan, I need to tell you—'

'Later,' he said, pressing a finger lightly against her lips. 'Don't worry about whatever it is. Everything will work out OK in the end. You have a flight to catch.'

And she hated herself even more for letting him talk her out of telling him. This was important. And the longer she left it, the more hurt he was going to be when she finally told him.

Please, please, don't let this be too much for him. Don't let it make him walk away from her. Don't let her lose him.

'You know you can call me any time,' he reminded her.

'Even if it's three in the morning, it doesn't matter—if you need me, just ring me.'

'I'm not going to disturb your sleep. But thank you. It helps to know you're there.' Her face was white. 'I love you with all my heart, Dragan.'

He stroked her face. 'Are you scared of flying, or something?'

Or something. 'I just want you to know that I love you.'

He smiled. 'I know. Just as I love you. And we're going to make that promise to each other in front of everyone the day you walk down the aisle to me.'

If he still wanted to marry her, once he knew the truth about her. 'Tell Reverend Kenner I'm sorry I couldn't make our meeting,' she said.

'He'll understand.' Dragan paused. 'Look—I won't ring you because it might be awkward timing for you. But call me when you can, OK?'

'I will.' She'd call him the second she got to Contarini.

And she'd tell him she loved him.

And she'd tell him what she was going home to. Exactly who she was.

'I love you. *Ti amo. Volim te,*' he added.

'I love you, too,' she whispered. '*Siempre.* Always.'

Dragan watched her as she walked through the scanner. All clear.

And then she was gone.

The way she'd kissed him goodbye had almost made it feel as if it was goodbye for ever. He pushed the thought away. Of course it wasn't. She'd be back in a few days. And maybe then he'd be able to take the sadness from her eyes, make her realise just how much she was loved. That it didn't matter if she didn't fit into her family, because she had him and their future children—and they'd be all the family she needed.

He drove home in complete silence. Parked in the road outside his cottage, lifted Bramble out, and let them both in. He had enough time to have a cup of coffee, make a fuss of the dog and change into a suit for morning surgery, and then it was time for work.

And right now Melinda would be on her way to London.

He walked over to the surgery. The village seemed to be busier than usual—clearly the tourist season had started early this year. Quite a few people had cameras. Well, Penhally Bay was picturesque, with the smattering of pagan memorials in the surrounding countryside, the wreck of the seventeenth-century Spanish treasure ship *Corazón del Oro* and the smugglers' caves, and the cliffs overhanging the Atlantic. Maybe these people were all from some camera club and they'd come to find inspiration for a competition or something.

'Morning, Dragan,' Hazel, the practice manager, said as he walked in.

'Morning, Hazel.' He smiled at her and headed for his consulting room. He'd just settled in when there was a rap at the door and Nick—as usual, without waiting to be asked—opened the door.

'Quick word,' he said—more of a statement than a question.

'Sure.' Dragan gestured to the chair next to his desk.

'We need to think about locums,' Nick said.

So now would definitely not be a good time to say he needed leave for a few days. Dragan carefully kept his expression neutral. 'We could do with a long-term one to keep us going through the summer. I know Adam's here now and he's taken over Marco's list, but we still need cover for Lucy while she's on maternity leave,' he said. And maybe longer, if Lucy decided she wanted a break before returning to medicine. 'We can just about manage for now, but we'll really need someone to help us next month when the tourists start arriving.'

'Good point. I'll get Hazel onto it,' Nick said. 'I did call to see you yesterday, but you were out. Interesting neighbour you have.'

'Cruella De Vil, you mean?' Dragan said before he could stop himself.

Nick's eyes widened in surprise. 'I thought she was rather fun, actually. We went out for dinner last night.'

'Uh-huh.' Dragan gave him a polite smile. Natalie or Natasha—or whatever her name was—wasn't his idea of fun. Nick was lonely, and Dragan could understand that, but why bother going out with someone so shallow when he could find himself someone genuine and warm? Someone more like…well, more like Kate, Dragan thought, the midwife who'd been their practice manager before Hazel had taken over.

'I'll see you later, then,' Nick said, and to Dragan's relief the senior partner left him to see his first patient.

Dragan just about managed to keep his mind on his work during the morning. But the second his last patient left his consulting room, he grabbed his mobile phone and checked it for messages.

There were two—both from Melinda.

In London. Love you. M.

Napoli. Love you. M.

It wasn't until after he'd finished his house calls that he had the text he'd really been waiting for.

Contarini. Love you. Call you soon. Something I need to tell you. M. xx

Something she needed to tell him? He frowned. She'd tried to tell him something earlier, but he'd told her it could wait. Well, whatever it was, it probably wasn't as bad as she thought. Things often seemed worse than they really were after you'd just had bad news.

Although he was itching to call her, see how see was, he

kept the desire under control. The last thing she needed was for him to ring her in the middle of something awkward. And at least he had something positive to do that evening. Knowing that Reverend Kenner liked dogs, Dragan was perfectly comfortable taking Bramble with him for a walk along the harbour down to the rectory, next to the church. Though it was with some relief that he passed Nick's house and saw that the senior partner's car wasn't there. He was probably out somewhere with that atrocious woman—which was a good thing. Then Nick wouldn't be asking just why Dragan was calling in on Reverend Kenner, who wasn't on his patient list. Until Melinda was back and wearing his ring, Dragan wasn't ready to discuss his plans with anyone else.

'Ah, Dragan. You've brought Bramble with you.' Reverend Kenner bent down to pat the dog. 'How's her leg?'

'This time round, hopefully, it's healing nicely. And I'm not letting her off the lead until we've got the X-rays back after her next check-up.'

'Would you like a cup of tea?'

English tea was one thing Dragan definitely hadn't learned to love. 'Thanks, but I'm fine,' he said with a smile.

'So, what can I do for you? You were quite mysterious on the phone.'

'Melinda's agreed to be my wife,' Dragan explained.

'Congratulations! I'm so pleased—you make a lovely couple. And people have been wondering, you know.'

Dragan smiled wryly. 'Nothing's ever secret for long around here, is it? Melinda would have been with me today, but she had a call from her parents last night and had to go back to Contarini. Her brother's been killed in an accident.'

'I'm so sorry. Do give her my condolences when you speak to her, won't you?'

'Of course.' Dragan paused. 'About the wedding—we wondered if you'd marry us in St Mark's.'

'I'd be *delighted*,' Reverend Kenner said warmly. 'Though you should expect the whole village to turn out.'

'That's fine by me. Um, I haven't done this sort of thing before, so I don't have a clue what the procedures are. I assume we have to fill in some sort of paperwork?'

'Yes. Strictly speaking, I *should* see you both together,' Reverend Kenner pointed out.

'Melinda will come to see you as soon as she's back in Cornwall,' Dragan promised.

'So have you any date in mind?'

'As soon as possible.'

Reverend Kenner raised an eyebrow. 'Should I be concerned about your reasons?'

Dragan shook his head. 'Not at all. It's just that now we've decided to get married neither of us wants to wait any longer than we have to. So what happens now? Do you read the banns or something?'

'Hmm.' Reverend Kenner frowned. 'Are you both British nationals?'

'I've spent nearly half my life here,' Dragan said, 'and I obtained British citizenship when I qualified as a doctor. But I'm not sure about Melinda.'

'Then we're probably safest to get a common licence—that's permission from the bishop for non-British nationals to marry here.'

Dragan blinked. 'We have to go and see the bishop?'

'We're quite a way from the bishop's diocese, but the good news is I'm one of the bishop's surrogates—I can sort out your application for the licence,' Reverend Kenner reassured him. 'I have copies of all the forms you'll need to fill out. You'll need proof of your nationality—your passport will do fine—and maybe a letter from the embassies saying that the marriage will be recognised in Melinda's home country.' He frowned. 'Is Contarini part of the European Union?'

'Probably.'

'If it is, I won't need a letter from the embassy, but check with Melinda. If it's not, I'll need the letter.' He smiled. 'I'm just so pleased for you both.' He checked in his diary. 'As soon as possible, you say. We need to allow a couple of weeks for the paperwork to go through, so we're looking at the end of the month... Ah, yes. We have a slot at three o'clock on the last Saturday in April, if that suits you both?'

'That'd be perfect.'

'You've sorted out your best man and bridesmaids?'

'Not yet. But now we've got a definite date, we'll work on it.'

Reverend Kenner handed him a sheaf of forms. 'Obviously we'll need to have a little chat—I always do with couples who want to marry—but it's nothing too onerous.'

'We don't mind,' Dragan said. 'We just want to get married. Properly.'

'And the whole village will be celebrating with you,' Reverend Kenner said warmly.

On the way home, Dragan remembered the hot-water bottle. Melinda had promised to return it to Violet Kennedy. Well, that was one small thing he could do to help: collect it and deliver it for her. It would give Melinda one less thing to worry about; being the conscientious vet she was, she was probably fretting about it. And she had enough to deal with right now.

The tourists were still hanging about outside the café—probably waiting for the sunset, he guessed. He unlocked the door to Melinda's flat, carried Bramble up the stairs, retrieved the hot-water bottle, and had just set the dog back on her feet and locked the door again when he realised he was surrounded. By the tourists. Who were busy taking photographs—of *him*.

'What's go—?' he began.

'So who are you to Princess Melinda?' one of them cut in.

'I beg your pardon?' He stared at the man. Princess Melinda? Was the guy talking about *his* Melinda?

'Princess Melinda. The heir to the throne of Contarini, now her brother's died,' one of the others said.

'Right stunner, she is. Blonde and...' One of the others lifted two hands, as if cupping curvaceous breasts.

They *were* talking about his Melinda. Dragan just about managed to contain the urge to punch him—no way was this grubby louse going to get his paws anywhere near Melinda!

'Give it a break, man. She's never going to look twice at you. Beauty, brains and royal, to boot—she's way out of *your* league,' one of the others said, nudging the mouthy photographer.

A camera flashed in Dragan's face. 'So you've got the key to her flat, then,' one of them said conversationally.

'I'm just a friend,' Dragan said. Though right now he was beginning to wonder. How could Melinda possibly be a princess and not have told him something so important about herself? She'd agreed to marry him, for goodness' sake. For better or worse. No secrets.

'Friend, hmm?' Another flash. 'So what's the hot-water bottle for?'

'It belongs to the owner of a patient she treated on call yesterday,' Dragan said shortly.

'And she didn't have time to return it before she went back to Contarini for the funeral?' one of the paparazzi said. 'Right. Good of you to help out. A *friend*, you say.'

'Hang on, you're the local doctor, aren't you?' another asked. 'Yes.'

'And you live just round the corner. Handy,' another one remarked.

How did they know he lived nearby? Had they been watching him?

'So what do you make of King Alessandro, then?' one of the others asked.

King Alessandro? Presumably he was Melinda's father. Dragan spread his hands. 'Can't help you, I'm afraid. Sorry. Excuse me.'

To his relief, they let him go, but his brain was whirring as he walked back to Fisherman's Row. Melinda was a princess? Heir to the throne, according to the paparazzi—and that meant she'd be Queen Melinda on her father's death.

And hadn't she said something about her father wanting to retire?

Oh, lord.

This changed everything.

He'd asked the local vet to marry him.

And it turned out that she was of royal blood. The heir to the throne.

No wonder she'd reacted so badly when he'd teased her about behaving like a princess—because that was exactly what she was.

But why hadn't she told him the truth about herself? Why had she lied to him? She'd agreed to marry him, yet she'd kept something this big from him. That didn't bode well for their marriage—if she'd be allowed to marry him in the first place. Her Royal Highness Princess Melinda Fortesque was hardly likely to marry a commoner. Especially when she was about to become Her Majesty, Queen Melinda.

Oh, hell.

Even if it was possible for her to marry him, they couldn't base a marriage on secrets and lies. No wonder she'd wanted to keep things low-key between them. It was nothing to do with avoiding being the top subject of the village grapevine— she'd probably been terrified that the press would ferret it out.

Well, they had now.

And if this was the 'something I must tell you'—she was too late.

* * *

Dragan's mobile phone—which he'd forgotten to take with him when he'd gone to see Reverend Kenner—was ringing as he walked in the door. He picked it up and glanced at the screen. Melinda.

What the hell did he say to her?

Although he was tempted to leave it and get his head round the situation before she called back, at the same time he needed to know the truth. From her. 'Hello?'

'Dragan? *Carissimo*, I rang and rang and you weren't there,' she said, sounding worried. 'Are you all right?'

No, he wasn't. 'Sure,' he lied. Even though she'd kept the truth about herself from him, she was in an awkward situation. Hundreds of miles away with a family who didn't accept her for who she was, preparing to go to her brother's funeral. Now wasn't the time to make a big deal out of it—though that didn't mean he was going to let her off the hook. 'Are you?'

'Sort of. But I miss you so much. Dragan, there's something I need to tell you.' She'd slipped into Italian and was speaking so rapidly that he had to concentrate to follow her. 'It's important and I know I should have told you before I left, but it was all such a mess, and there was no time, and I'm sorry, and...' She paused for a moment. 'Dragan, about my family. There isn't an easy way to say this, so I'll say it straight. My father's the king of Contarini.'

'King Alessandro. I know.'

Melinda was stunned. He *knew*? But who'd told him? 'How?'

'I went to get Violet Kennedy's hot-water bottle from your flat to take it back to her and save you the job, and the paparazzi were there when I came out.'

'And they hassled you? Oh, no!' He must be so hurt and angry—learning that she'd kept this from him for so long. And hearing it from someone else instead of from her...

'Dragan, I'm so sorry. I really didn't want you to find out that way. I wanted to tell you myself.'

'Bit late now.' He was clearly trying to keep his voice toneless, but even he could hear the hurt and anger seeping through.

'Are you all right? The paparazzi didn't—'

'It doesn't matter about them,' he cut in. 'Why didn't you tell me before?'

'Because I couldn't find the right words. I know I should have told you. But I was…' She paused, trying to find the right word. One that wouldn't make things even worse. 'I was scared.'

'Scared?'

'That I'd lose you.' She dragged in a breath. 'Once people know I'm Princess Melinda, they treat me differently. And I didn't want things to change between us.'

'You think I'm that shallow?'

'No, of course I don't! But it's human nature that people see the title—it gets in the way of seeing the person. I didn't want to lose you, lose what we have. All I wanted was to live a normal life, just like any other person.'

'But you're not just any other person, are you? You're next in line to the throne. You're the heir in waiting.'

'Yes and no.'

'What's that supposed to mean?'

'Officially I'm the heir at the moment. But I don't want to be queen. And I'm not going to be either.' She swallowed. 'My father wants to retire—abdicate, call it what you want. He's got high blood pressure, so it's sensible that he starts to take things easier now he's older. And at least nowadays there is the option to abdicate—in the old days he would have been king until he died and the job would have killed him. If he hands it over to me…then he's free. It will be better for his health.'

'So you're staying in Contarini.'

'No.' She bit her lip. 'I don't belong here, Dragan. I belong in Penhally, with you. I'm just Melinda Fortesque, the local vet. And I'm getting married to the love of my life.'

His silence told her that he didn't believe her. That he was hurt and angry and didn't know how to trust a single word she said.

She hadn't actually *lied* to him.

But then again, she hadn't told him the whole truth either. And lies of omission were still lies.

'Dragan. I love you, I love Penhally and I love my job. I don't want to be the Queen of Contarini. I don't want to run the kingdom. I have no interest in politics and I'd be a rubbish head of state. I'm not what Contarini needs.'

'What about your duty to your family?'

He'd stayed in the village in Croatia during the war to pay off his family's debts—debts that hadn't been their fault at all—to make sure his family honour stayed intact. He'd put his duty before his own safety. And in her shoes she knew he'd do the dutiful thing. He'd give up the woman he loved and the job he loved for his family's sake.

But her family wasn't like his.

And giving up the life she loved to be the Queen of Contarini would be the biggest mistake she'd ever make.

She had to convince him of the truth. 'I'm not the only child. My younger sister Serena's everything I'm not—she enjoys politics and diplomacy, and she's good at it. She'd make a brilliant queen and she'd love every second of it. Whereas my heart won't be in it, and that would make it wrong for me and wrong for the country.' She closed her eyes for a moment. 'I have to do the right thing, Dragan. The right thing for everyone.'

'So that means it's over between us.'

'No! I'm still the same woman I was when you asked me to marry you.'

'Are you? Melinda, you're of royal blood. You're never going to be allowed to marry a commoner.'

'Yes, I am.'

'And then what? If you're married to a commoner, the law means you can't become queen?'

She sucked in a breath. Did he really think…? 'I'm not using you to get out of being queen, if that's what you're thinking. *Dio*—I fell in love with you, Dragan, almost the first moment I saw you. You're everything I want in a man. Apart from the fact that I go up in flames every time I look at you, it's who you *are*. You're honest and you're honourable and you do what's right. You're compassionate and you're kind and you're clever and I…I'll be so proud to be your wife. And I'm stuck here, hundreds of miles away from you, where you can't see my face or my eyes and know for yourself that I mean every word I'm saying, that I'm not lying to you or using your or…' She swallowed hard. 'Look, I'm coming home. I'll call you from the airport and let you know when my flight's due in.'

'Melinda, you can't. You went back to Contarini for your brother's funeral,' he reminded her.

'Which is tomorrow.' She closed her eyes for a moment. 'And it's going to be horrible. My parents didn't let me say goodbye to him in private. Saying goodbye in public isn't the same.'

'I know, but you still need to say goodbye. Or you'll feel there's unfinished business.'

Was that how he felt? Had he even had the chance to say goodbye properly to his family? She hadn't asked—and she couldn't ask now, not without ripping his wounds open again. She'd hurt him enough today—enough for a lifetime. 'I'm sorry,' she whispered. 'This is all such a mess.'

'Go to the funeral, Melinda,' he said softly. 'You owe it to yourself and to your family. Don't turn your back on them.'

'I…'

'Things will work out, Melinda. For the best.'

He sounded all calm and reassuring, but there was an undercurrent. An undercurrent that told her he was having doubts—about her, about the way she felt about him. She needed to get back to Penhally and straighten this out. She'd stay for the funeral, but then she'd be on the first possible flight back to England. She'd go home to the man she loved— and make him see that she loved him. 'I'm coming home as soon as I can after the funeral,' she said. 'We'll talk when I get back.'

'Sure.'

'I love you, Dragan. And I'm so, so sorry.'

'Uh-huh.'

He hadn't said he loved her, too. Her stomach turned to water. Please, don't let her lose him. Don't let him walk away from her under some misguided notion that he was helping her do the right thing—because ruling the country would be so very much the wrong thing for her and for Contarini. 'And, Dragan? About the press—'

'I told them I was your friend,' he cut in. 'Your neighbour.'

'They drag things up,' she said. 'So don't believe whatever you read in the papers or what they say to you. It might not be true. There might be a spin on it to make a story. And don't let them rile you either—just smile politely and say "No comment" to absolutely everything, and they'll leave you alone pretty quickly because they'll realise they won't get anything. Otherwise they'll hound you and push you into doing or saying something you'll regret. But I'll be home soon and I'll take the heat off you. I promise. And I love you.'

'OK.'

One tiny word. Two syllables. And it was untrue: everything was very far from being OK.

And he hadn't said he still loved her.

She had to get home to Penhally and fix this.

Fast.

CHAPTER SEVEN

DRAGAN was halfway through his breakfast the following morning when his mobile phone beeped.

Melinda.

He flicked through to the message.

Am flying home tonight. I love you. M x

He loved her, too. But he'd spent a lot of the previous night thinking. And he still didn't have any answers. It was her duty to go back to Contarini and rule. Her family needed her. But he would have no place in the life of Queen Melinda: he was standing in her way. It wasn't fair to make her choose between him and her family. He was going to have to do the honourable thing.

Even though the thought of losing her ripped his heart into shreds.

Be thinking of you today. D x, he texted back.

His phone beeped again within seconds. *I miss you. M x*

He missed her, too. But playing text-tennis wasn't going to help either of them right now. *Due in surgery. Turning phone off now. D x*

As soon as he left the house, he saw the paparazzi. And he was well aware that he was being followed all the way to the surgery.

There were stares from the patients, little speculative

murmurs and whispers behind hands as he walked in to the waiting room.

'Well, well. You and Melinda,' Hazel said, a knowing look on her face.

Oh, great. So Nick had spotted him last night, leapt to conclusions and speculated in the staffroom. Just what he could do without this morning. 'What did Nick say?'

'Nick?' She looked surprised. 'Nothing. He's too busy with that pushy bottle blonde to notice anything.' She shook her head. 'That woman's no good for him.'

'He needs someone with a heart,' Dragan agreed.

'Someone like our Kate. She's such a lovely girl.'

'Absolutely.' Dragan's smile was genuine; he liked the midwife. 'Though maybe we shouldn't be matchmaking.'

'Matchmaking.'

Uh-oh. Wrong choice of word. He'd clearly just reminded Hazel about a choice piece of gossip, because the practice manager tapped the side of her nose. 'You kept it quiet about Melinda.'

He sighed. 'Because we both prefer things to be private. Not that there's much chance of that around here,' he said ruefully. 'And the village grapevine's not on form because that's very old news.'

'No, not about you two seeing each other. Everyone's known that for *ages*,' Hazel said impatiently. 'I mean about who she really is. Of course, the papers got some of it wrong because it's not a secret about you two around here.'

Papers?

Even as it sank in, she fished under her desk and handed him the paper. The headline was enormous.

ROYAL VET'S SECRET LOVER

Underneath, there was a picture of him—a photograph that had clearly been taken outside Melinda's flat the previous evening.

'I had no idea she was royalty,' Hazel said, looking interested. 'I mean, she's always had that air of quality about her, but I thought she was the Penhally vet.'

'She is,' Dragan said. 'Hazel, forgive me for being rude, but I really don't think this is the time or place discuss this.' And he most definitely didn't want any speculation getting back to the paparazzi. 'Excuse me. I'm keeping everyone waiting. I'll be ready for surgery in five minutes.'

He managed to field awkward questions from his patients, but the paparazzi were still there when he left the surgery at lunchtime, posing as tourists: sitting at one of the little pavement tables outside the café, looking out to sea or reading a newspaper; browsing in the window of the surf shop or the little souvenir place; apparently studying the collection times listed above the post box set in the post-office wall.

If he ignored them, they'd probably follow him to all his house calls and compromise his patients' confidentiality. But he couldn't *not* do his house calls and compromise his patients' health.

Just smile politely and say 'No comment' to absolutely everything, and they'll leave you alone.

He'd never had to deal with the press. So he'd have to rely on Melinda's advice for this one.

For the first time ever, he found himself sympathising with the celebrities who complained about the invasion of their privacy. He'd had barely a day of it, but it was already grating on his nerves.

'What's wrong with these people, Bramble?' he asked. 'I'm just an ordinary man.'

The problem was, his girlfriend wasn't ordinary.

He gave the paparazzi polite smiles but said nothing as he lifted Bramble into the back of his car, although he realised before he'd driven to the end of Bridge Street that he was being followed on his way out of the village. Part of him was tempted to lead his pursuers on a wild goose chase and lose them in the maze of narrow Cornish lanes with their high stone walls. But then again, Melinda had said that if he didn't react they'd realise there was no story. So let them follow him. They'd soon find out what a GP's life was like. And it wasn't the media version of a doctor raking in the cash and dumping their patients on an out-of-hours call system either—at Penhally Bay Surgery, they did their own calls.

He noted after his first three calls that his pursuers tended to hang about in gateways with maps—obviously they could pretend to be lost tourists if anyone challenged them. But he forgot about them completely when he did his fifth call of the afternoon, at the riding stables a few miles south of Penhally.

Georgina Somers came out to meet him. 'Thanks for coming, Dr Lovak.' She leaned through the car window to stroke Bramble. 'Hello, you. So when are you going to be fit enough to chase rabbits again, then?'

'Soon. Provided she doesn't overdo it and skid round a corner and crack the bone again, like she did the last time I let her off the lead.' Dragan smiled at her. 'So what can I do for you, Georgina?'

'It isn't me.' She kept her voice low. 'It's Luka. I'm worried about him.'

Dragan frowned. Luka was one of the stablehands, who lived in a caravan tucked away in a quiet corner of the stable grounds. George Smith, Melinda's boss, had always said that Luka was brilliant with horses and he'd give him a job like a shot. 'What's wrong?'

'He says he's just got a virus, that's why he's got a sore throat and a bit of a temperature. But I'm not so sure. He caught himself on some barbed wire last week. He says I'm fussing, but he just doesn't look right and nobody else has come down with a sore throat and a temperature. I think it might be blood poisoning or something because he wouldn't let me treat his hand last week either.' She sighed. 'I know, it's awful of me to call you out for a cut hand—but you know what Luka's like.'

Along with the rest of his family—Romany travellers—Luka Zingari was incredibly suspicious of the medical profession. And out of all of the doctors at the Penhally practice, Dragan knew that he was the one they were most likely to respond to: the stranger in a strange land, like them. 'I'll have a word with him,' he promised.

'I'll take you over.'

Was this just a concerned employer worrying about her stablehand? Dragan wondered. Had Georgina's father called him, it would be more a case of an employer worrying about being sued—Malcolm Somers was very much of the old school and believed in paying his staff as little as possible for the maximum amount of work. Malcolm had finally handed over the running of the stables to his only child the previous year—although he interfered all the time, according to Melinda.

Something about Georgina's expression alerted Dragan. It wasn't the face of a concerned employer. It was more like a girlfriend who was worried sick.

Were Georgina and Luka…?

He chided himself even for thinking it. Who was he to speculate? Especially as the press were speculating about him and Melinda. He should know better. It was none of his business. But it would explain a lot.

Georgina rapped on the caravan door. 'Luka? It's me. Can I come in?'

There was a muttered croak from inside the caravan, and she opened the door. 'I know you said not to fuss, but Dr Lovak's here. He was calling on Mum…' her quick glance pleaded with Dragan not to expose the lie '…and when I told him you'd been ill he asked if he could drop in.'

'I don't need a doctor. She's fussing,' Luka said.

But the sardonic grin on his face worried Dragan. Luka was a typically handsome gipsy—again according to Melinda, half the girls in the village fancied him—and that grin definitely wasn't his normal expression.

An alarm bell rang in his mind. Luka worked at the stables. He'd cut his hand on barbed wire. If Luka's tetanus vaccinations weren't up to date, that could be a pretty nasty combination. 'So how are you feeling?' he asked.

'It's just a virus. Sore throat, headache, bit of a temperature. It'll go.'

'But you're having problems swallowing.'

'Only because of my sore throat.'

'Then you won't mind me checking your pulse, will you?' Before Luka could protest, Dragan checked the pulse at his wrist. 'Your heartbeat's pretty rapid.'

'Because I've got a bug.' Luka rolled his eyes. 'Georgie's fussing.'

'Have you had any pains in your arms or legs or stomach?'

'It's just a bug.'

Dragan knew Luka was going to evade any other questions along that line, so he changed tack. 'How's that hand you hurt the other week?'

'Fine.'

'Can I take a look?'

Luka looked at Georgina, sighed, then held out his left hand. Dragan gently unwrapped the slightly grubby bandage. 'Have you put anything on this?'

'It'll heal.'

Dragan raised an eyebrow. 'Well, I reckon you've got a bug all right.'

'See?' Luka glanced at Georgina. 'I told you it was all right.'

'Actually, it's not. You haven't got flu. It's a bacteriim called *Clostridium tetani*,' Dragan said.

'Oh, lord. You mean he's got *tetanus*?' Georgina looked shocked.

'When was the last time you had a tetanus vaccination?' Dragan asked Luka.

'No idea. I don't like needles,' Luka admitted.

'Most people don't. But it's not worth taking the risk of skipping a vaccination, especially with what you do for a living. Stables are one of the most common places to find *Clostridium tetani*.' Dragan looked at him grimly. 'Get a puncture wound from a nail—or in your case have an argument with some barbed wire—and then muck out a stable, and the bacterium's just found its dinner.'

'So what does tetanus do—*if* I have it?'

Lord, the man was stubborn. Even more so than Melinda.

'It's a disorder of the nervous system. It gives you muscle cramps—and that sometimes makes it hard to open your mouth, which is why tetanus is also known as lockjaw. In the early stages, you might get muscle spasms around the site of the infection—but when it hits the bloodstream it tends to affect your facial muscles,' Dragan explained.

'So when the bug's out of my system I'll be fine.'

'That's the thing,' Dragan said softly. 'If you don't treat it, you're pretty likely to die.'

Luka blinked. 'You what?'

'You're likely to die,' Dragan repeated. 'And it's not a nice way to go. You can't breathe properly, your muscles go into spasm and you suffocate. Or maybe the next muscle to go into spasm is your heart—it stops, and that's it. We probably won't get you back because your heart muscle won't respond to being shocked. Then there are your kidneys, there's the possibility of septicaemia… So you need treatment, Luka.'

'You don't know I've definitely got tetanus.'

Dragan had met Luka before and knew the man wasn't being awkward just to be macho—the chances were that Luka was terrified of hospitals, and denying that anything was wrong with him meant he wouldn't have to even consider the idea of going near one.

Georgina clearly thought the same, because she begged, 'Make him see sense, Dr Lovak. Luka, if I lose you...'

Luka's right hand reached out to grip hers. 'You're not going to lose me.'

'Then you need treatment, Luka,' Dragan said softly. 'You need to go to hospital. For Georgina's sake, if not your own.'

Luka shook his head. 'I'm not going in an ambulance. They're meat vans.'

'You don't have to go in an ambulance. I'll take you myself,' Dragan offered.

'I hate hospitals.'

'So do a lot of people. But you've got a three in five chance of dying if you don't have treatment.'

'Which gives me a two in five chance of being fine. Forty per cent's reasonable odds,' Luka said.

Dragan shook his head. 'This is going to get a hell of a lot worse before it gets better. *If* it gets better.'

'What does the treatment involve?' Georgina asked.

'I'm not going to lie about it. It involves needles. But you'll need some antibodies against the bacteria, Luka—they're called tetanus antitoxins. And some antibiotics, as well as something to stop your muscles going into spasm. This kind of treatment's best done in hospital, where there's a sterile environment.'

Luka scoffed. 'You see it in the paper all the time, people going into hospitals and catching a superbug because the place isn't clean.'

Luka's caravan, although small, was absolutely spotless.

'Often things make the news simply because they *are* news, not the norm. You need medical attention, Luka. Attention I can't give you.' Dragan sighed. 'As well as the medication, they're going to need to get plenty of protein into you and a lot of calories to fight the infection, so they'll probably put you on a drip. Once the needle's in, it doesn't hurt, and it's the best way to get the right fluids into you.'

'So you're saying I'll have to *stay* in hospital?' Luka's eyes widened.

'It won't be for that long.'

'No. No way. I belong *here*.'

He'd heard that before. Very recently. From someone just as stubborn.

Except she wasn't here now.

'I belong with the horses,' Luka insisted.

'Then the sooner we get you to hospital, the sooner we can get you back here with the horses again.'

Luka was silent for a long, long time. Only the way he gripped Georgina's hand gave any clue to what was going on in his head. Finally, he looked at Dragan. 'All right. I trust you.'

Melinda hadn't. The thought skidded into Dragan's mind before he could stop it. He pushed the idea away. Now wasn't the time to start thinking about the way his life had been turned upside down. He had a duty to his patients. 'Let's go, then,' he said quietly.

'Can I come with you?' Georgina asked.

'Better not,' Luka said. 'Your dad will go mad. You're not even supposed to be seeing me. And with your mum ill…She doesn't need the stress of your dad in one of his moods.'

'Dad's just going to have to accept it,' Georgina said, lifting her chin.

'His daughter moving in with what he calls a "dirty bloody gyppo"?' Luka shook his head. 'Don't push it, Georgie. You don't break a horse by smashing its spirit. You get it to trust you and work with you as a partner, so you're a team.'

'And you think you can make Dad change his mind?'

'It just takes time. Softly, softly. The more he gets to know me, the more he'll realise that true Romanies aren't thieves or liars or unclean—that he's got the wrong idea.'

'Dad never admits to being wrong.'

'He will this time.' Luka squeezed her hand. 'I'm not going to kiss you. I don't want you to get this. But everything's going to be all right.'

The irony wasn't lost on Dragan. It was the same situation as his own: Malcolm Somers, the owner of the riding stables, might just as well be the king of Contarini. Just like Melinda's father, Malcolm Somers wasn't going to want his daughter seeing someone he considered to be of inferior social status.

Whether Luka would be able to work a charm offensive on Malcolm and make the older man realise that there was no disgrace—that Luka was Georgina's equal and would treat her with the love and respect she deserved—Dragan didn't know. But he seriously doubted that he'd be able to do that with Melinda's family. Which meant they'd cut her off. She'd be isolated from her family.

So he was going to have to do the right thing and let her go. Let her be what she was born to be: a princess.

CHAPTER EIGHT

DRAGAN wasn't answering his phone. Melinda frowned. He'd probably left it at home while he took Bramble for a walk. *Dio.* She missed the dog pattering around. She missed holding Dragan's hand while they strolled down to the cliffs. She missed Cornwall. And, oh, how she missed Dragan.

But soon she'd be home. And she couldn't wait to see him. She quickly tapped in a message. *On way home. Will call you from Newquay.*

'Your Highness, are you sure about this?' the pilot asked when she boarded the small plane. 'Your mother…'

She smiled at him. 'Don't worry. She'll be angry with me, but I'll make sure you won't get into trouble. I just want to go home.'

The pilot gestured out towards the airfield. 'Contarini is your home, Your Highness.'

She shook her head. 'Not any more. Please, can we go?'

'No, you jolly well can't,' a voice said from the doorway. 'You're supposed to say goodbye first.'

'Rena! What are you doing here?' Melinda asked, surprised to see her sister.

'Just making sure you're all right.' Serena boarded the plane and sat next to her sister. 'Are you sure you're doing the right thing? This isn't…a…well…'

'Fling?' Melinda supplied.

The pilot withdrew to a discreet distance.

'No.' Melinda was very definite. 'Dragan is the love of my life. For the first time I can ever remember, I belong somewhere. With him. And I want to be with him, Rena.'

'Well, if his personality's as gorgeous as his looks…'

'It is,' Melinda confirmed.

'And he makes you happy?'

Melinda nodded. 'Happier than I've ever been in my life.'

Serena hugged her. 'Then follow your heart. I wish you both all the best. And I'm most definitely coming to the wedding—and I expect to be a bridesmaid—so you ring me as soon as you've sorted out a date.'

Melinda bit her lip. 'I don't think *Mamma* and *Papà* will be there.' Her mother had expressly decreed that morning that there would be no wedding. And Melinda had finally snapped, telling her mother a few things she should have said years ago.

The ensuing row had practically blistered her ears.

They'd presented a united front at the funeral, for the sake of the media. But Viviana Fortesque had made it very clear that if Melinda went back to Cornwall it should only be to sort things out. 'And then you will come back here, to your rightful place. You are next in line to the throne,' she'd said coldly. 'And you know your father needs to abdicate, to take things easier and leave the running of the kingdom to someone else. You *cannot* walk away from your duty.'

What about her duty to her patients, to her colleagues? Melinda refused to leave them in the lurch. And, most of all, she refused to leave Dragan. And she'd made that just as clear to her mother—who'd responded with the stoniest, iciest silence Melinda had ever encountered.

'*Mamma* will calm down. In a week or so,' Serena said. '*Papà* will talk her round, like he always does.' She grinned.

'Though I never thought I'd see the day you got the headlines above Raffi.'

'It's not funny, Rena. The timing was atrocious.' And it had taken every ounce of backbone she'd had that morning, to face her mother's fury as she'd banged the newspaper onto the table. ROYAL VET'S SECRET LOVER

'*Mamma* would've had a fit whatever day she'd seen that headline,' Serena said wryly. 'Though yes, today was probably not the best of days for it to happen.' She hugged her sister. 'Be happy, Lini. And I'll speak to you soon. Let me know you've arrived safely.'

'I will. And thank you, Rena. For being there.'

'It's how families are supposed to be,' Serena said softly. 'How I wish ours had been when we were growing up. And how I hope yours will be now.'

So do I, Melinda thought. So do I.

The flight back to England seemed interminable. But finally they landed. As soon as she was through customs, she rang Dragan. And how good it was to hear his voice.

'I'm in Newquay. I missed you so much, *amore mio*.'

'Do you want me to come and pick you up?'

'Better not—there are paparazzi everywhere.' And she didn't want her reunion with Dragan all over the front pages. She wanted that to be very, very private indeed. 'Have they been bad to you?'

'They've followed me everywhere. But I took your advice: I just smiled and said nothing.'

'Good. We'll draft a statement to the press and it will quieten down.' She bit her lip. 'Dragan, I'm so sorry it happened like this.'

'You can't change the past.'

He sounded calm, but she could hear the hurt seeping through his stoicism. 'I'm still sorry. Because I never meant to hurt you.' She paused. 'I'll sneak into yours the back way, yes?'

'Won't they follow you?'

'Believe me, I've had a lot of practice in avoiding them,' she said dryly. 'I could have a PhD in it by now.'

'I'll leave the French doors unlocked.'

'Thank you.' She paused. 'Dragan? *Volim te.*'

'I'll see you soon.'

Hell, hell, hell. If he wasn't responding when she used his own language…this was going to be hard. Knowing Dragan, he was still thinking about her duty and he was putting distance between them to make it easy for her to go back to Contarini.

But that wasn't what she wanted.

She'd fight for her man.

Because he was worth it.

The drive back from the airport dragged on and on and on. But finally the taxi drove into Penhally—and how good it was to see the bay spreading out in front of her. *Home.*

The driver dropped her by the Higher Bridge; she knew that the paparazzi, even if they had information that she was on her way back, would be camped outside the veterinary surgery and she would be shielded from their view by the houses in Gull Close. Any other photographers would be stationed at the front of Fisherman's Row; they wouldn't expect her to cut round the back of the houses in Bridge Street and through the little alley at the back of Dragan's house.

She could see him sitting at the table in front of the French doors, reading some medical journal or other. And just the sight of him made her catch her breath. She tapped softly on the glass, then opened the door, locked it behind her and closed the curtains. Just in case.

And then she was in his arms. Holding him so tightly, as if she'd never let him go again.

She had no intention of ever letting him go again.

'*Volim te.* I've missed you so much.' She reached up to draw his head down to hers, brushed her mouth against his.

She could feel a reserve there—well, he'd learned the truth about her in the worst possible way, so of course he'd be hurt and wouldn't quite be sure of her—but please, please, just let him kiss her back. Let him give her the chance to show him exactly how she felt. Skin to skin, body to body, no barriers between them. Let her tell him without words how much she loved him, make him believe the truth: that she was completely his and nothing was ever, ever going to change that.

She pulled back slightly to look into his face. His dark eyes were unreadable. 'Dragan?'

'I'll put the kettle on.' He untangled himself from her arms.

The kettle? She hadn't seen him for days, he hadn't kissed her back, and he was talking about making a cup of *coffee*?

This wasn't the man she'd left in Penhally.

And she wanted her man back. Right now.

She followed him to the kitchen and, after checking that the blinds were drawn, slid her arms round his waist and rested her cheek against his back. 'I've missed you, *zlato*.'

Gently, he prised her arms away.

'Dragan? What is it?'

He turned round to face her, leaning back against the kitchen worktop. 'I can't do this.'

'Can't do what?' Ice began to trickle down her spine.

'You and me. I…don't think this is a good idea.'

She stared at him. 'But…only a few days ago you asked me to marry you.'

'I asked our local vet to marry me,' he corrected her. 'But you're Princess Melinda. A stranger. I don't even know what I should be calling you. Your Majesty? Ma'am? Your Royal Highness?'

'Ma'am and Majesty are for queens. And don't you *dare* start on that "Highness" rubbish. It's an accident of birth that my parents are who they are. I'm just Melinda. The same as you've always called me.' She dragged in a breath. 'I haven't changed, Dragan.'

'Yes, you have,' he corrected quietly. 'Because I don't know you at all. The woman I asked to marry me—I thought I knew her. But I was wrong. You're a princess.'

'I'm sorry. I *know* I should have told you the truth about me, a long time ago. I should have prepared you properly for what it would be like, not left you to the mercy of the paparazzi. I just didn't think they'd be here so soon. Stupid of me.' She shook her head. 'I just want to be like any other woman. I want to marry the man I love. Work among people I care about. Be *myself*.'

'But you have duties, Melinda. Responsibilities.'

Now, this she'd expected. She'd prepared her arguments. 'I've talked to my parents about this. I'm not going to be queen. This stuff with the paparazzi—it'll last a few more days, maybe, and then it will all go away and we can get on with our lives as normal.'

'But what's normal?' he asked.

'You and me. Penhally. Seeing patients. Matching up our call lists so we can grab half an hour to ourselves at lunchtime.' She shook her head. 'Dragan—look, I know I hurt you and I'm sorry for that. I know I was wrong not to trust you with everything—but it isn't you. It's my own stupid fault, for being too scared that you'd walk away if you knew who I was, for letting my fears blind me to the kind of man you are. I didn't want to lose you—I *don't* want to lose you.' She gritted her teeth. 'I hate this royal stuff. I always have. When I was younger, it was like growing up in a fishbowl. I couldn't open my mouth or do anything without people analysing what I did or said—and most of the time they put completely the wrong interpretation on it. Every mistake I made, the press blew it way out of proportion. I couldn't do anything like a normal person, and the paparazzi were there every minute of every day, telephoto lenses poking into my life.'

Dragan could understand that. He'd had a taste of that the past few days.

'Everything I did was in the public eye,' Melinda continued. 'And my days were one long round of protocol, protocol, protocol. Even when I knew someone was a devious, lying snake and I wouldn't trust them a millimetre, I had to be gracious to them at official receptions or it would turn into a diplomatic incident and undo years and years of work.' She shook her head. 'No, it's not a fishbowl, it's a straitjacket. I loathe politics and all the politeness and the lies and the spin and the protocols. That's not the world where I want to be.'

But it was the world she'd been born into.

'I can't live in your world, Melinda.'

'My world is *your* world,' she said softly.

'How? I'm the village doctor here in Penhally and you're a princess—the heir to the throne of a Mediterranean island.'

'I haven't called myself "princess" in years.'

'That doesn't stop you being one.'

'I've never felt like a princess, Dragan.' She took a deep breath. 'You told me about your family…now let me tell you about mine. You want to know the truth, why I don't talk about my past? Because I was unhappy, and I don't want to dwell on all that misery.'

Her eyes were sparkling with anger and pain, and he could tell just how strongly she felt because her accent had deepened. 'My parents were always distant, too busy with affairs of state to see what was happening with their children. My brother Raffi was left to grow up like a wild child. When he was just fifteen, he was photographed by the paparazzi in a bar, drinking alcohol, despite being way under the legal age limit. It snowballed from there. He followed our Uncle Benito—my father's younger brother—in being a playboy, except Benito at least worked hard to balance it out. Raffi…well, he just laughed and said it didn't matter, because he was the heir to the throne and the favourite and he'd do whatever he liked.' She spread her hands. 'He had no self-discipline, no thought for others. Which was why he ended up wrapping his car round a tree last week. Thank God he was the only one involved and didn't hurt anyone else.' She shuddered. 'I think that's why my father didn't suggest abdicating before—because he knew Raffi was too young and irresponsible to make a good king.'

Dragan looked at her. 'You're the heir to the throne now. And you have the self-discipline your brother lacked.' Studying for a degree in veterinary sciences wasn't an easy option, and doing it in her second language would have made it even harder.

'But I don't have the rest of the princessy accomplishments. I was never the elegant young debutante who was happy with her ballet lessons and piano lessons and deportment and whatever else a princess is supposed to learn—the only thing I enjoyed out of that lot was riding, and that was only because I could escape to the stables and could learn how to look after the horses. The number of times my mother dragged me out and told me that I shouldn't be playing around in all the mess—how I should act like a princess instead of having straw in my hair like a stablehand. And I couldn't do it. I never fitted in.' She sighed. 'You know, most girls spend their time dreaming they're princesses in disguise—like the princess and the pauper. For me it was the other way round. I wanted to be the ordinary girl, not the princess.'

That was what she'd been when she'd met him. An ordinary girl. The newcomer to the village—a stranger in a strange land, like himself.

But all the time she'd been playing a part. Pretending to be someone she wasn't.

Was she playing a part now? He couldn't help wondering.

'You're not an ordinary girl. You're Princess Melinda of Contarini.'

'I'm Melinda Fortesque, MRCVS. Soon to be Melinda Lovak.' She paused. 'Unless you've changed your mind.'

It was breaking his heart to do this, but he had to do the right thing. Families were important, and he couldn't let her cut herself off from hers. 'It can't happen. I don't fit into your world—and you know it, or you would have asked me to go with you.'

'You think I asked you to stay because I was ashamed of you?' She shook her head. 'Far from it. I'm *proud* of you. But you have to understand, my mother is a cross between Queen Victoria and Attila the Hun. She's a terrible snob. I didn't want her being rude to you and hurting you.'

'Your parents are never going to accept me,' he pointed out softly. Just as Georgina's parents would never accept Luka. Different class, different culture.

'They *will*.'

Typical Melinda. Stubborn. But for her own sake he had to make her face the truth. 'So how did they react to that newspaper story?' he asked.

'Not well,' she admitted.

'Exactly. No way will they let you marry a commoner.'

'I don't want to marry some prince or other they've chosen for me. I want *you*,' she said.

'The papers brought out all the stuff about me being a refugee.'

She spread her hands. 'So? Dragan, it wasn't your fault there was a war. And you have nothing to be ashamed of. Nothing! You had a horrible time that wasn't of your making, but you came through it. You've worked hard and you've made something of yourself. You haven't just taken and taken—you've given back. You're a good man. And that's exactly what I told my mother. That you're kind and compassionate, that you're a brilliant doctor, that you're clever—for goodness' sake, you were going to study law and you speak more languages than I do! I told her that every day is better for me now when I wake up because I know you'll be there. I love you, Dragan.'

She paused and looked straight at him.

He knew what she was waiting for. And how he wanted to tell her that he loved her all the way back. That, yes, he felt hurt and angry and betrayed that she'd kept the truth from him, but they'd work it out together because he loved her.

But he had to do the right thing. Which meant denying it.

'I can't forgive you for keeping me in the dark—for agreeing to marry me when you know it can't happen.'

'Yes, it *can*.'

How? They were worlds apart. And Melinda was destined to rule her country. 'Marry me, and you'll cut yourself off from your family.'

She raked a hand through her hair. 'Dragan, I know family's important to you. I know you miss yours. And if mine were even the slightest bit how you described yours to me, there wouldn't be a problem. But they're not. And I've barely been back to Contarini since I came to England to study veterinary science. My parents didn't even come to my graduation. That's how close we are. So cutting myself off...' She shrugged. 'There's nothing *to* cut off. My sister's the only one I'm close to, and I don't really fit into her social circle either.' There was the tiniest sparkle in her eye. 'Though she liked your picture in the paper. And she told me to follow my heart.'

Follow your heart. Good advice. Except...sometimes you had to put your duty first. Melinda's father was ill and needed to retire. Her family needed her—and in his eyes family should always come first. He knew she was planning to put him before her duty—which was wrong, wrong, wrong. Whereas if she thought there was nothing for her here, it might make it easier for her to leave. To go back and do the right thing.

For her sake, he was going to have to say something that hurt him bone-deep. 'We're not getting married,' he said. 'It's over.'

Her eyes widened. 'No. You don't mean that. Please, Dragan. Tell me you don't mean it.'

'I can't marry someone who doesn't trust me. Someone I don't trust any more.'

'But, Drag—'

'It's over,' he said, not looking into her eyes because he didn't trust himself not to crumble. 'I'm sorry. You'd better leave through the back door—there are paparazzi out the front.'

She stared at him for a long, long moment.

Then she left the room. Closed the French doors behind her.

And Dragan discovered that the pain he'd known as a teenager, when he'd lost his family, had just come back. With a vengeance.

CHAPTER NINE

YEARS of training let Melinda walk down the little alley at the back of Dragan's house and through to the other side of Harbour Road with her back straight and her expression neutral. Even though she wanted to bawl her eyes out, she made absolutely sure that the paparazzi couldn't detect her thoughts—no way was she going to let them have a picture they could use with a speculative caption.

But the second she was back in her flat with the door closed behind her, she slid down the wall to the floor, drew her knees up to her chin and wrapped her arms tightly round herself.

It was all over.

Dragan had called off the wedding.

Now he knew who she was, he didn't want to know—her worst nightmare had just come true.

As she'd told him, if you were royal and you made a mistake, it would be all over the papers. Talked about. And just when people had started to forget, the whole thing would suddenly blow up again. It would go on and on and on.

She could see the headlines now. DR LOVE-AK DUMPS PRINCESS

About the only people who'd be pleased about it were her parents.

But it didn't change things. Even if Dragan didn't want her, she still had a life here in Cornwall. And she wasn't going back to rule Contarini.

'Backbone,' she reminded herself. 'Keep it straight.' *Like a princess*. And she was well aware of the irony.

She picked up the phone and dialled her boss. This was another call that was way overdue. Someone else she'd lied to by omission. 'George? It's Melinda.'

'How are you, love?' he asked.

My heart's just cracked right down the middle. 'I'm fine,' she lied. How could he be so nice to her when she'd behaved so badly? 'And, George, I'm really sorry that you've had a hard time from the press.'

He laughed. 'Once they realised that the only time I'd talk to them was with my arm up a cow's backside and plenty of manure around, it rather put them off.'

'Even so. I'm sorry. I really should have told you who I was. As my boss, you had a right to know.'

'You had your reasons.'

She had.

Her boss was a damn sight more understanding about it than the love of her life had been. But, please, don't let this princess business have wrecked her job, the way it had wrecked her relationship with Dragan. Dragan hadn't even been able to look at her; he'd never be able to forgive her for hiding the truth from him. For not trusting him when she should have done. 'Do I still have a job?' she asked in a small voice.

'Of course you do. Being a princess doesn't get you out of your job without at least a month's notice, you know.'

His tone was light and teasing, but she could hear the warmth and concern in his voice and it hurt. Because right now she felt so alone. So isolated. So *empty*.

'Then I can come back to the surgery tomorrow morning?'

'Bright and early, usual time,' he said. 'You'll be pleased

to know Cassidy's ready to go home tomorrow and he's back on his usual diet. We had a bit of a scare with him while you were away, but Jake sorted us out. He's a good contact to have for exotics. Well done, you.'

'I didn't exactly do much.' She'd brought the parrot into the surgery—and then she'd abandoned him along with the rest of her job and caught the next flight to London. Some vet she was.

'You treated the bird before he was too far gone to help. If you'd left it until the morning, he wouldn't have made it and Violet would have a broken heart. Don't do yourself down, love.' He paused. 'Or should I call you Your Highness from now on?'

She strove for lightness. 'Melinda will do just fine.'

'I'll see you tomorrow, then, love.'

'See you tomorrow, George. And thank you.' She cut the connection, replaced the phone, took an apple from her fruit-bowl and headed down into the practice.

Cassidy perked up as soon as he saw her. ''Ow do, m'dear?'

'Pretty rubbish, actually,' she told him.

The parrot swore a blue streak, and she smiled wryly. 'Saves me doing it, I suppose. But I was meant to be teaching you something nice.' She made a kissing noise. '*Ti amo, tesoro.*'

The bird responded with something pithy.

She cut him a piece of apple with a scalpel and fed it to him. '*Ti amo, tesoro.*'

This time there was no response at all.

She checked that he had enough water, scratched his poll just the way he liked it—and clearly he'd picked how to purr like a cat since he'd been in the surgery—then walked out of the room. As she turned off the light, she heard a very quiet kissing sound. '*Ti amo, tesoro,*' Cassidy informed her.

Something Dragan would never say to her again.

And somehow she had to learn to live with it.

Kate walked through the door of the practice a moment after Dragan the following morning. She looked hot and bothered, although she didn't appear to be out of breath; he had a feeling that her high colour was due to anger rather than rushing. 'What's up, Kate?' he asked.

Kate pulled a face. 'Nick and that wretched clippy-clop woman.'

'Clippy-clop?' Dragan asked, mystified.

'The one who thinks it's practical to wear high-heeled mules in a Cornish seaside village.' Her scowl deepened. 'Horrible woman. She dresses at least fifteen years too young, too. Nick must be going through the male menopause to think it makes him look young, having *her* on his arm. Maybe she looks young from a distance—but up close you can see she's trowelled on her make-up to cover up the lines.'

Nick had never, ever heard Kate make a bitchy remark about anyone; their former practice manager, who'd recently done a refresher course and returned to the practice as a midwife, was always calm and unflappable and friendly. He stared at her in surprise. 'What did she do?'

'Oh, nothing. Just made some stupid remark about Jem's name, and I shouldn't let her get to me.' She flapped a hand. 'I was just taking Jem to meet Mum in the café—it's the school holidays and she's looking after him while I'm here this morning—when we bumped into them outside the post office. She couldn't have got much closer to Nick if she'd stripped off the little she was wearing.'

Kate wasn't normally that vehement or judgemental; then again, she was very protective of her son. Which didn't surprise Dragan that much, as she was a single parent and Jem was all she had. 'Natasha's staying in the holiday cottage next to me,' he remarked.

Kate rolled her eyes. 'Oh, don't tell me *you* think she's gorgeous, too.'

'No,' Dragan said mildly.

'Good. At least one of the men around here has some common sense, then.'

'Don't be too hard on Nick. He has his faults but he has a good heart.'

Kate pulled a face. 'Well, at the moment he's acting like an *idiot*.'

There was much more to this than met the eye, Dragan was sure, but he didn't push it. He hated people interfering in his life, so he'd give Kate the space she clearly needed.

Kate grimaced again. 'Hazel, I'm sorry I'm late. Give me three minutes and I'll be ready.' She patted Dragan's arm. 'Sorry for being grouchy. Are you all right? Those photographers must be making your life hell.'

He shrugged. 'I'll survive.'

'Well, if you need to escape, you know where I am.'

He smiled ruefully. 'And then the headlines will no doubt claim I'm cheating on Melinda with you. Thanks for the support, Kate, and I really appreciate the offer—but I'm not going to put you or Jem through that.'

'With any luck they'll find someone else to bother soon.'

'With any luck,' he agreed. But he knew it was going to run for a bit longer yet—and either way he was going to come out of this badly. Either the papers would denounce him as the love rat who'd dumped the princess, or they'd denounce him as the loser who wasn't good enough for the princess and she'd dumped him.

He managed to get through the morning's calls, deflecting all speculation and questions with a smile and bringing the conversations right back to his patients' health worries, but in the afternoon he was called out to Mrs Harris, a neighbour of the Chamberlains.

'I was cycling home from my friend's when I saw her milk was still out on the front doorstep. So I went round the back and found her,' Tina explained. 'She's fallen and she says her leg hurts.'

'Don't move her,' Dragan said. 'But get a blanket and put it over her to help keep her warm. I'm on my way.' Mrs Harris was one of his patients, and he knew she had osteoporosis. The chances were she'd cracked at least one bone and she'd need X-rays and hospital treatment. St Piran Hospital was a half-hour drive away; although he could drive her there himself, given her condition it would risk making her injuries worse, and she'd find the ambulance much more comfortable. He rang through to the ambulance station and explained the situation, agreeing to call them from her house if her injuries weren't as severe as he expected.

But the examination confirmed his worst fears. 'You've broken your hip,' he said gently. 'I'm going to give you some pain relief now, but you need to be treated in St Piran.' And, given her osteoporosis, fixing the fracture could turn out to be a real problem. Not that he was going to worry her about this now. 'An ambulance is on its way.'

'Hospital? But I can't! What'll happen to Smoky?'

The cat—which was almost as elderly as Mrs Harris—was sitting in her basket. She lifted her head on hearing her name and miaowed softly.

'We could take her in and look after her until you're home again,' Tina suggested.

'That's sweet of you, love, but she's terrified of dogs. No, I'll have to stay with her.'

'You need to go to hospital, Mrs Harris,' Dragan said gently. 'You need specialist treatment, something I can't do for you here.'

'I can't leave Smoky,' Mrs Harris said stubbornly.

'Leave this with me,' Tina said, and pulled her mobile phone out of her pocket.

Dragan assumed she was going to call one of her friends and concentrated on treating Mrs Harris, examining her to make sure he hadn't missed any complications and to make sure she wasn't going into shock from loss of blood, then giving her pain relief.

It was only when the door opened and he heard a soft voice saying, 'Hello, Mrs Harris. Now, Smoky, shall we reassure your mum that we can find you somewhere nice to stay while she's in hospital?' that he realised who Tina had called.

Melinda.

Every nerve-end was aware of her. And how desperately he wanted to hold her close.

He glanced up. 'Ms Fortesque,' he said, as coolly as he could.

'Dr Lovak,' she responded, her tone equally cool.

She scooped up the cat and sat on the floor with Smoky on her lap, near enough for Mrs Harris to be able to touch her cat.

Yet more proof of why she was a brilliant vet. She understood her patients *and* their owners and she was sympathetic to both. When she left to rule Contarini, she'd leave a huge hole behind in the community as well as in his heart.

'How long will you need to stay in hospital?' Melinda asked.

'Dr Lovak says it depends on how long it takes to heal,' Mrs Harris said, her voice slightly shaky. 'Am I going to be stuck on a bed in traction?'

'Not with your hip—it's usually treated by an operation,' Dragan said. 'The ambulance is already on its way, and they'll take you to the emergency department at St Piran. They'll give you an X-ray to see what the break looks like, and then they'll decide how best to treat it. They might put a special pin in your thigh bone to fix it, or they might have to replace the head of your thigh bone with a special metal head. Or if the break is very bad, they might need to replace your hip completely. But they'll get you up on your feet again as soon as possible, walking with a frame, and as soon as they think you're able to look after yourself, they'll let you come home again.'

'They won't put me in a home?' Mrs Harris bit her lip. 'Nursing homes don't take pets, and I can't be without my Smoky.'

Dragan took her hand. 'They won't put you in a home,' he said. 'The occupational health people will come out to see you, but not to put you in a home—they'll want to see what help they can give you to make life easier, especially while you're recovering. They can fit rails and change the height of your chair to make it easier for you to get out of it.' They'd also check the flooring and the layout of the house to reduce the risk of her falling again, Dragan knew. The important thing was to make sure that Mrs Harris didn't lose any of her confidence or independence; they didn't want her ending up trapped in the house. 'And Lauren from the practice will come and see you about physiotherapy to help you get your leg working properly again.'

'Lauren's lovely—she's really kind. And don't worry about Smoky,' Melinda said. 'I know several people who don't have dogs who would be able to look after her for you until you're back.'

'And I can come in and help you with Smoky when you're home again,' Tina said. 'Mum and I will keep an eye on your bungalow until you're home, and I'll call the milkman and sort everything out for you.'

'And I'll take pictures of Smoky in her holiday home and

bring them to show you in hospital. That's the difference between Penhally and the city,' Melinda said, giving Dragan a speaking look. 'People here *care* about others.'

That one had been aimed specifically at him, he knew.

He cared all right.

But he was trying to do the right thing for Melinda's family. Putting her before his own wants.

Determined not to rise to the bait, he concentrated on re-assuring Mrs Harris until the ambulance arrived, then gave a handover to the crew, telling them what he'd given her and advising them about her osteoporosis.

Tina locked up. 'I'd better get back, or Mum'll be worrying about me.'

'Thanks for all your help,' Dragan said. 'You were brilliant.'

'And I'll let you know about Smoky,' Melinda said, gently putting the cat into a travelling basket.

And then it was just the two of them.

There were dark shadows under her eyes. She'd clearly slept as badly as he had last night. 'How are you?' he asked.

'I feel as bad as you look.'

Straight and to the point. That was his Melinda.

Except she couldn't be his Melinda any more. 'I'm perfectly fine,' he lied.

'You are *such* a liar.'

He coughed. 'Isn't that the proverbial pot calling the kettle black?'

'I've already apologised for that. It was wrong of me not to tell you the truth. But what you're doing right now is just as wrong. Dragan, you know we're right together. I love you and I know you love me. Why torture us like this?'

'Because,' he said, 'sometimes you have to put your duty first.'

She shook her head. 'My future is with *you,* not in Contarini.'

'And your family? You're just going to abandon them when they need you?'

'No. There's a way through all this. We just have to find it.' She bit her lip. 'So what do I tell the press? They're expecting an official statement.'

'Tell them you're going back to Contarini.'

'No.' She looked exasperated. 'Dragan, I love you, but right now you're driving me crazy. The best way for me to protect you from the press is to give them a statement, otherwise they're going to keep following you and hounding you until you crack.'

'You said they'd go away when they realised they wouldn't get a story from me.'

She grimaced. 'They will—but they'll try their hardest to get their story first.'

'Then tell them it's over.'

'That's the thing about a newspaper story. "Who, what, where, when and why?" They've already got the who, where and when—that's us, here and now. If we give them a "what"—that we're not together—that leaves one question unanswered. "Why?" And they won't rest until they've got an answer.' She spread her hands. 'So telling them it's over is only going to make things worse. And it's also not true anyway.'

'It's *over*,' Dragan repeated.

'Look me in the eye and tell me you don't love me any more,' she challenged.

He looked away. 'I don't love you any more.'

'Yes, you do,' she said softly. 'Dragan, you're hurting both of us. I understand you're angry with me for keeping things from you. I messed up. But how long are you going to make both of us pay for my mistake?'

'It's not just that. How do I know you're not keeping anything else from me?'

'I'm not.' Her eyes narrowed. 'So you're saying you don't trust me any more?'

'Right now,' he said quietly, 'I don't know what I feel. Except mixed up. A few days ago everything was simple. Now it's a minefield. Whatever I do suddenly has all sorts of consequences. I'm in a world where I don't belong.'

'I don't belong there either.'

'You were born into it,' he reminded her. 'That is who you are.'

'No, it isn't.' She sighed. 'This is getting us nowhere. Dragan, when are you going to see—?'

His mobile phone rang, cutting into her question.

'I'm on call,' he reminded her. He glanced at the screen. 'It's the surgery.'

'A patient needs you.' She frowned. 'You'd better answer that. We'll talk about this later, when we have more time. *Ciao.*'

CHAPTER TEN

DRAGAN didn't ring Melinda that night. He didn't want another of those circular arguments; right now he needed some space. Time to think.

Bramble lay at his feet, nose on her paws, staring at the door and clearly waiting for Melinda to appear.

'I know I'm hurting you, too, and I'm sorry,' Dragan said ruefully. 'But she's not ours any more. I was stupid to let her close to us in the first place—I should've learned by now that if you let people too close, you lose them. And somehow we both need to learn to stop loving her.'

The dog blew out a breath, and continued staring at the door.

Melinda didn't ring him—clearly realising that he needed some time—and Dragan spent most of the night watching the minute hand on his alarm clock drag slowly round. When he got to the surgery the following morning, tiredness meant he wasn't in the best of tempers.

'A word,' Nick said, leaning against the doorjamb.

I'm really *not* in the mood for you this morning, Dragan thought, but forced himself to smile at the senior partner. 'What can I do for you, Nick?'

'All this royal stuff. I'm worried that it's going to affect the practice.'

'It's not going to affect the practice.' So far today the paparazzi had left the surgery alone. But that might be because they were camping outside the veterinary surgery, he thought wryly.

'I just want to make sure that nobody's going to have any problem doing their job.'

The holier-than-thou attitude stuck in Dragan's throat. And before he could stop himself, he snapped, 'I'm not the one who affects the practice by screwing up relationships with the staff.'

'What's that supposed to mean?' Nick demanded.

'Get your own house in order before you start trying to organise mine.' Dragan knew he should shut up, and shut up now—but the pent-up anger of the last few days was too much for him. 'That girlfriend of yours, Natasha, is upsetting the staff every time she expects them to be her personal secretarial service. And look at the way you behaved towards Ben and Lucy, look at how things were between you and Jack—and I bet they're not much better between you and Edward. Then there's the way you never date anyone more than half a dozen times, with the excuse that you don't want to get close to anyone after you lost Annabel.' He ignored the fact that he'd made exactly the same decision after losing his family. 'Do you really think she'd want you to live like this?' Dragan shook his head. 'You're brilliant with patients but your personal life is a complete mess, so *don't* you tell me what to do, Nicholas Tremayne.'

Nick's jaw dropped and he just stood there, clearly lost for words and looking shocked.

Probably because Dragan was always quiet and professional. Well, today he'd had enough of being quiet. He'd had enough, full stop.

'Now, if you will excuse me, I have patients to see. And we are trying to stick to our ten-minute slots, are we not?'

To Dragan's relief, Nick took the hint.

Though he also banged Dragan's door very hard as he left.

The morning surgery calmed Dragan's temper, and by the

end of his session he was feeling thoroughly guilty. He'd overstepped the mark. Big time. He checked on the computer that Nick was free, then walked across the corridor to the consulting room opposite his and knocked quietly on the door.

'Yes?' Nick snapped.

Dragan opened the door and leaned against the doorframe. 'I owe you an apology. What I said was out of order. Your personal life is none of my business.'

'Apology accepted.' Nick raised an eyebrow. 'Though it's the first time I've ever known you lose your temper.'

'I'm sorry. It was unprofessional of me.'

'It was human,' Nick said, surprising him. 'You've been under a hell of a strain these last few days. And you can't exactly go and punch one of the paparazzi or the pictures will be splashed all over the tabloids.'

'Sadly, Nick, you're absolutely right.' Dragan shrugged. 'It'll die down. I'm only sorry that it's making people's lives a bit difficult around here.'

'Hazel told me one of them had been in here the other day, giving her a hard time—and you sorted it out. Thank you.'

'It's my job,' Dragan said. He wondered if Hazel had also let slip about Kate's reaction to Natasha—a reaction that had made Dragan wonder just what the midwife's feelings were about Dr Nicholas Tremayne.

'Even so. I should've been here.'

'You weren't on call,' Dragan pointed out. 'And you were busy with, um…' He just about managed to stop himself using Kate's nickname for the woman—or the one he'd bestowed himself, Cruella De Vil.

'Going to lecture me again?' Nick asked.

'No. All I will say is that families are important. And I don't think someone that shallow and self-centred will fit in with Lucy and Ben or Jack, Alison and Freddie.'

Nick didn't correct him, Dragan noticed. So clearly he

knew what Natasha Wakefield was really like. He looked thoughtful. 'Anyone would think you have someone else in mind for me.'

Someone like Kate with her warmth and her calm, common-sense attitude towards life. Though Nick would probably deem her not glamorous enough. And it wasn't any of his business anyway. Dragan shook his head ruefully. 'With the mess I've made of my own personal life, I'm in no position to give advice.'

'I think,' Nick said wryly, 'you were right about what you said this morning. I'm not giving advice either. Except I could do with a pint and a spot of lunch—and you look as if you could do with one, too. Smugglers Inn?'

'I have house calls this afternoon,' Dragan said.

'They sell non-alcoholic beer.'

It was an olive branch. Probably one he didn't deserve. So, despite the fact it was something he wouldn't normally do— he couldn't even remember the last time he'd had lunch with Nick—Dragan nodded. 'You're on.'

'We'll look out to sea and set the world to rights. *Without* the complication of women,' Nick said.

Melinda stared at the computer screen in dismay.

Bramble was on her list of patients for the late afternoon surgery.

And although she adored the dog—she'd been the one to rescue the flatcoat retriever in the first place—right now she had a major problem with the dog's owner. He was being so pig-headed, and even though she could understand why he was behaving that way, it drove her crazy. Half a dozen times the previous night she'd picked up the phone and started to punch in his number. But every time she'd stopped part way through and replaced the receiver. Pushing him would only make him more determined. Maybe he needed time to miss her as much as she missed him—so much that it physically hurt. He'd talk to her when he was ready.

She just about managed to get through the first three cases on her list. Check-up and first vaccination for a kitten, followed by an annual booster and a check-up for a springer spaniel called Rusty who had a slight heart murmur.

'I can hear it,' she said when she removed the stethoscope from her ears, 'so I think it's upgraded to a three rather than a two, as it was last time.' Heart murmurs fell into six classifications: anything up to three was fine, but more than that needed medication.

The owner looked dismayed. 'But he hasn't seemed ill. I would've brought him in if I'd noticed anything different. He pants a bit in the evenings, but no more than he used to.'

'Any coughing?' Melinda asked.

'No.'

'OK. Just keep an eye on him—if he's panting more or he starts coughing, then we know he's struggling. You can help relieve some of the strain on his heart by keeping him on the lean side.'

'I know our last spaniel was overweight, but we've been careful not to give Rusty any snacks between meals.'

'You're doing fine,' Melinda said. 'He's not overweight at all. But being a little tiny bit lighter—say a kilogram—will make it a lot easier on his heart.' She checked the dog's teeth and ears, then made a fuss of him. 'Well, Mr Beautiful. You can take your owner home now.' She smiled up at the owner. 'You're doing a great job with him. He's a lovely, lovely dog.'

Next up was a dog who'd been limping. She showed the owner the claw that had almost curved back into the pad of the dog's foot.

'What's happened here is that this tendon doesn't work properly, so his toe's lifted up and the claw doesn't come into contact with the ground when he walks,' Melinda explained.

'You'll need to keep an eye on the toe and either bring him here for clipping, or do it yourself when you check his dew-claws.'

'Is it going to hurt?' the owner asked.

'No, it's like clipping your own fingernails—though obviously if you go too far you'll hurt him. Most of them don't like it, so I'd suggest it's a two-person job. And give him lots of praise and a reward afterwards.' She talked the owner through the procedure. 'Slip the nail into the opening here, keep reassuring him, try to distract him a bit, and—there. Done. He might limp for a day or two, but that's because he's sore from the claw going into his pad—having the nail clipped hasn't hurt him. But if you don't like the idea of doing it yourself, you can always bring him in. Just keep an eye on the claw because it needs cutting before it starts to touch the pad.'

'Thank you so much.'

And then she had to face Dragan and Bramble.

It was a real effort to be professional when all she wanted to do was run into his arms and tell him how much she missed him, how much she wanted him back.

'How are you?' she asked.

'Fine.' There was a pause. 'You?'

'What do you think?'

He didn't answer, but he looked incredibly embarrassed. Obviously he realised she was 'fine' in the same way that he was. As in *not*. Melinda wasn't sleeping, she wasn't eating, and she was as miserable as hell.

She forced herself to be professional. Bramble was, after all, her patient. 'How's Bramble? I see she's not limping as badly.'

'No.'

'Still lifting her?'

'To be on the safe side.'

Bramble's leg had been slow to heal, and then the dog had

chased after a rabbit. When Dragan had called her back, she'd skidded, twisted slightly, and then had been in such obvious pain that Melinda had X-rayed the dog and discovered the movement had loosened the pins in her leg and the bone had cracked again.

'Would you like to lift her up onto the table?'

He did so, and Melinda felt the dog's leg. 'No flinching or guarding—that's good. And the wound has healed nicely.'

Bramble licked Melinda's face, and Melinda swallowed hard. 'Ah, *bella ragazza*, I miss you, too. I miss going for walks along the harbour with you. I miss having you curled on the sofa with me while a certain person is doing paper-work. I miss feeding you scraps of chicken in the kitchen when I'm cooking and he can't see me sneaking you a treat.' She gently stroked the dog's head. 'I wonder, does he miss it, too? Does he find the bed's way too wide, that the seconds drag, that the sun's stopped shining?'

'Melinda.' Dragan's voice sounded tortured. 'Don't do this.'

So he missed her, too.

Good.

With any luck, he'd come to his senses soon and stop making both of them so miserable.

'One more X-ray, I think,' she said. She ruffled Bramble's fur. 'I know you hate needles, *carissima,* but this is just one tiny, tiny one to sedate you for the X-ray and make you comfortable.'

A second later it was done. She carried Bramble over to the X-ray area. 'I'll have the results back tomorrow.' And it was a brilliant excuse to talk to him.

'Hopefully she'll be fine and the next time you see her will be for her booster vaccination,' Dragan said.

'The next time I see her in a professional capacity, you mean.' The words were out before she could stop them. She rubbed a hand over her eyes. 'Sorry. But I miss her.' And she missed him. 'Dragan. We really need to talk about this.'

'Not here. You have a queue of patients building up.'

'After surgery, then. Are you on call tonight?'

'No. Are you?'

'Yes.' She walked over to her desk and pressed it hard. 'But, touch wood, we'll have at least some time to talk. Is half past seven good for you?'

He nodded. 'Your place or mine?'

'Neither. Let's escape from the paparazzi. You know that little pub we used to go to?' The one just outside Penhally where they'd met up in the early days of their relationship, when they had still been keeping things quiet from the village grapevine.

'OK. We'd better take separate cars,' he said. 'In case you're called out.'

'And if we both take different routes, it should put the paparazzi off our trail.'

'Fine. I'll see you then.'

For a moment she thought he was going to kiss her goodbye. He even swayed towards her. But then he pulled back without touching her. 'Thank you for seeing Bramble.'

'*Prego.*' She bit back her disappointment. She couldn't expect too much, too soon. But maybe tonight, when she'd talked to him, he'd understand. He'd hold her. And they could start taking those important steps back towards each other.

As soon as Melinda pulled into the car park that evening, she saw Dragan. He'd opened the boot of his car and was sitting on the bumper, making a fuss of Bramble.

The man she loved.

The man she wanted to be her family.

Her heart felt as if it was doing a back flip when she saw him smile at the dog. Please, please, let him smile at her again. Let things go back to how they'd been before Raffi had died.

'What can I get you?' he asked.

'In a moment. Let's walk on the beach first.'

Bramble's tail wagged madly at the word 'walk', and Dragan just about caught her before she jumped out of the car. 'Steady, girl,' he said softly.

They walked down the rocky path to the bay; once, Melinda stumbled, and Dragan automatically put a hand out to steady her. She wasn't quite sure how it happened, but then they were holding hands. And it felt so good, she wanted to cry with relief. Maybe they still had a chance. Maybe she hadn't wrecked this completely.

She didn't say a word, not wanting to break the spell and make him pull his hand away from hers. And, to her relief, the beach was deserted. Everyone was probably having their evening meal in the pub.

They stood in silence near the edge of the lapping waves, looking out to sea. When Bramble flopped onto the sand, Melinda smiled and dropped to a sitting position, tugging Dragan down with her.

Although in some respects she didn't want to break the silence, she knew they had to get this out in the open before they could move on. 'I've been thinking,' she said softly. 'I know you think I have a duty to go back. And I know you think I'm being selfish.'

'Aren't you?'

She turned to face him. 'Dragan, I know you'd give anything for the chance to be able to go home and help your family. That they came first with you. But the difference is, your family loved you right back. And they wouldn't have expected you to give up being a doctor for them.'

'I was going to be a lawyer,' he reminded her. 'And then manage the family firm.'

'But supposing you'd hated boats? Supposing you'd discovered…oh, say, that you were a brilliant artist? Your family would've encouraged you to follow your dreams. To follow your vocation, yes?'

'Yes,' he admitted.

'There's the difference. My parents never did. They only ever noticed me when they wanted me to do something for them. Right from when I was very small, I wanted to work with animals. I wanted to be a vet. And I've worked hard to make it happen.' Her jaw tightened. 'Only my *nonna* understood that. Remember I told you that my parents didn't even come to my graduation? They treat me as if I'm a spoiled child who's just playing dress-up—that this is some kind of *hobby* for me.'

He shook his head. 'You're a professional, and you're good at it. But the thing is, Melinda, there are other people who can do your job. There aren't other people who can rule Contarini.'

'Actually, there are.' She dragged in a breath. 'Do you want to know what I spent last night doing—apart from trying very hard not to come over and see you? I read the constitution of my country—I got Serena to scan it and email it to me. And there are ways around this. My father could pass an act of parliament so the title goes to his brother instead of to me. Or I could be crowned and then abdicate—and then Serena can take over, because she's next in line after me.'

'Have you asked Serena how she feels about that?'

'She was born to be queen, Dragan. She's everything Raffi and I weren't. She's diplomatic, she's good with people—'

'You're good with people,' he cut in.

Melinda shook her head. 'Not in the same way.'

'All the same, have you asked her?'

'Not *exactly*,' she admitted.

'So aren't you just doing the same as your parents? Expecting someone else to fall in with what you want?'

She felt the colour burning through her cheeks. 'I'm not being manipulative, Dragan. Of course I'll talk to Serena about it—it has to be what she wants, too. And if she does…then there's no reason why I can't stay here. With you.'

'And if she doesn't?'

'Then it's back to the drawing board. We'll think of something else.' But at least he was still holding her hand. Her fingers tightened around his. 'Is it so much to ask? Just to live my life like any other woman, be with the man who makes me feel as if I really belong somewhere for the first time I can remember?'

He was silent for a long, long time. Finally, he raised their joined hands to his mouth and kissed the back of her hand. 'I don't know. I would always put my family first, do the right thing. But, as you say, our experiences are different.' He paused. 'And I'm still trying to get my head round the fact that you didn't trust me.'

'I *do* trust you, Dragan. I just panicked—I acted with my head instead of my heart. I remembered the way people had reacted to me in the past, and although I know you're not like any of them I couldn't help myself.' She grimaced. 'The irony is now you don't trust me.'

'Can you blame me? Our whole relationship was based on secrets and lies.'

'Not lies,' she corrected. 'There was one thing I hadn't told you.'

'I'm very glad,' he said dryly, 'that you didn't call it "just one little thing". Because it was a *big* thing.'

'I know, and I'm sorry. But it was the *only* thing I didn't tell you.' She held his gaze. 'And everything else I've told you has been the truth.'

'The truth, the whole truth, and nothing but the truth?'

She smiled wryly. 'Yes. And I'd swear that in a court of law. I never wanted to hurt you, Dragan. You mean everything to me.' She swallowed hard. 'So where does that leave us?'

'This whole thing has hurt us both,' Dragan said, 'so let's just take it slowly. Get to know each other again. This time no secrets.'

'No more secrets. I promise,' she said.

'*Bene.*' He kissed the back of her hand again.

She coughed. 'Up a bit.'

He shook his head. 'Too soon. We're taking this slowly.'

'And that means what…dating?'

'It means taking it slowly and learning to trust each other,' he said, standing up and pulling her to her feet. 'Come on. Time to go back.'

CHAPTER ELEVEN

'SLOWLY' meant frustratingly slowly, Melinda discovered. She'd drafted a statement for the press, with Dragan's agreement, that they were 'just good friends'. Which meant that in Penhally they couldn't even hold hands or kiss each other goodnight. In a way, it went with Dragan's insistence on taking things slowly, getting to know each other again—but she ached for their old, more physical relationship. She missed waking up in his arms, having breakfast with him.

Well, maybe not so much breakfast.

She'd lost her appetite, and even the scent of toast had turned her stomach.

Or maybe it was her period coming. She'd always been peculiarly sensitive to smells just before—

She stopped dead.

No.

She couldn't possibly be pregnant. She and Dragan had only made love without protection that one time—the night before she'd gone back to Contarini. And it had been her safe time. Some couples tried for years and years to get pregnant; the chances of her falling pregnant on just that one night were low.

All the same, she couldn't shift the thought from her head.

Thank heaven today was Saturday and she was only working in the morning—which meant she could drive out to Newquay in the afternoon, where she could be safely anonymous. There was something she most definitely didn't want to buy in the village—the last thing she needed right now was gossip.

After surgery, she deliberately took a route through the back roads, knowing she'd be able to lose the paparazzi in the high-walled narrow lanes with all their twists and turns and little by-roads—months of living and working here meant she knew the roads so well that she no longer needed the map she kept in the glove box. Once in Newquay, she parked and browsed through a few shops, just in case she was still being followed. The second she was sure she was alone and unwatched, she bought a pregnancy test in the supermarket. The little cardboard box felt as if it was burning a hole in the boot of her car all the way back to Penhally. And she was careful to keep a very tight hold of her shopping bags when she carried them up to the flat—if she dropped them and the test spilled out, the paparazzi would go bananas.

Results in one minute. Just what she needed.

She read the instructions swiftly and did the test. And watched as the first line turned blue: good, the test was working.

And then she watched in horror as a blue line appeared in the second window.

Positive.

She was pregnant.

Expecting Dragan's child.

Oh, *Dio.*

Two weeks ago, if someone had told her she and Dragan were going to have a baby, she would have been shocked but delighted. But now life was a whole lot more complicated. Her relationship with Dragan still wasn't quite what it had been before she'd returned to Contarini, and she wasn't sure how he'd take the news. Would it make things right between them again when he learned that they were going to have their own family?

And then there were her parents. She had no idea how they would react to the news. Would her mother be like a normal grandmother, forgive everything the second she held the warm weight of the baby and breathed in that special newborn scent? Or would her parents decide she was bringing shame on her royal lineage—for being pregnant and unmarried?

And when the press found out about this they'd have a field day.

She needed to tell Dragan first.

But she needed to know for sure before she told him. Because this would really rock his world—they hadn't talked about having children, so she had no idea how he'd react. Delight at the idea of having a family of his own again? Or would it send him running scared?

She had to take this carefully.

Maybe the test was wrong. Maybe she'd done something incorrectly.

Luckily she'd bought a double pack. She drank water. Lots of it. Repeated the test. And watched the two blue lines slowly, slowly appear.

OK. Definitely pregnant. But *how* pregnant?

There was one person who might be able to tell her. One of her best friends in the village was a midwife: and Melinda knew Chloe would be discreet. She dialled the number. It rang and rang, and Melinda was just about to give up when she suddenly heard a familiar voice. 'Hello?'

'Chloe? It's Melinda. Um, are you busy?'

'Nothing I can't can a break from. Are you all right?'

'Ye-es. I don't really want to talk about this on the phone.'

'Got you. I'll be there in a minute.'

'You're wonderful. Thanks. I'll put the kettle on.'

But when Chloe arrived and noticed that Melinda was drinking water rather than coffee, she raised an eyebrow. 'This isn't just a girly chat, is it?'

'No,' Melinda admitted. 'Though can you promise me you won't say a word to anyone?'

Chloe's eyes widened. 'Of course I won't! Apart from patient confidentiality, you know I'm not like that.'

Melinda winced. 'I'm sorry. I know you won't. I didn't mean to…to make you feel bad. It's just this paparazzi thing getting to me and my mouth isn't acting in synch with my brain.' She dragged in a breath. 'I'm pregnant, Chloe.'

'Are you sure? When's the baby due?'

'I don't know. That's what I was hoping you might be able to tell me.'

'When was your last period?' Chloe asked.

'Two weeks ago.'

'Then you can't be pregnant, Melinda—you're only halfway through your cycle.'

'That's what I thought. But lately I've been feeling as if I want to howl my eyes out—and I've never been the leaky tap type.'

'You're under a lot of stress right now,' Chloe reminded her, 'what with your brother dying and these photographers following you about. It's not surprising you want to cry.'

'And I've been feeling sick. And I'm off my food.'

'Also symptoms of stress,' Chloe said calmly.

'And my sense of smell—it's much stronger than usual.' Melinda grimaced. 'The thing is, Dragan and I… We took a risk once. The day before I went to Contarini. So I did a pregnancy test, just in case.'

'And?'

Melinda took the test sticks from the worktop and handed them to her friend in silence.

Chloe stared at them. 'These are just as reliable as the ones I can do, so that's pretty conclusive.' She took Melinda's hand and squeezed it. 'Well. Congratulations.'

'I hope. Things still aren't that good between me and Dragan. We're taking it slowly.' Melinda swallowed hard.

'And you know what they say about people having a baby to patch up a relationship. It never works.'

'Firstly, that's not why you're having this baby. And, secondly, Dragan loves you. He's just a bit…well…mixed up at the moment. Not that I've said anything to him.'

Chloe was a total sweetheart and she'd never interfere, Melinda knew.

'I need to tell him. But not until I know for sure how pregnant I am.'

Chloe looked thoughtful. 'Your last period…was it lighter than usual?'

'Yes.' Melinda frowned. 'Now I come to think of it, the last two were a bit light.'

'Some women have a very light bleed for the first couple of months—it's all to do with hormones settling down,' Chloe said, 'so you could be three months gone already. Did you have any spotting before the first light period?'

'I'm really not sure. Why?' Melinda went cold. 'Does that mean there's a problem?'

'No, it just happens sometimes as the egg implants into the lining of the womb,' Chloe explained. 'Nothing to worry about at all.'

'Can you do a scan?'

'We don't have the equipment at the surgery. You'll have to go to St Piran for the ultrasound,' Chloe said. 'I can get you an appointment—and because you're not sure of your dates and you might be three months already, they'll fit you in pretty quickly. I'll ring first thing on Monday morning and book you in—that is, if you want me to be your midwife?'

Melinda hugged her. 'I'd *love* you to be my midwife—you're one of my best friends and I know I'll be in safe hands. Thank you, Chloe. I really appreciate this.'

'Hey. That's what friends are for.' Chloe hugged her back. 'Don't worry. Everything's going to be fine.'

Maybe.

But Melinda still felt the prickle of doubt all the way down her spine.

No more secrets.

Guilt flooded through Melinda. But this wasn't a secret, exactly. Nobody knew, apart from Chloe—who wouldn't say a word. Melinda was going to tell Dragan as soon as she knew when the baby was due. She'd make sure the time and the place were right—and she'd tell him.

But even so, she found herself picking at her meal when she went to a restaurant not far from Penhally with him on Sunday night.

And he noticed.

'Are you all right?' he asked.

'Just not that hungry,' she prevaricated, pushing her plate away. 'Sorry. I'm just a bit tired.'

'I'll pay the bill, then walk you back.'

It wasn't exactly far. Just round the corner.

'Do you want to come in for a coffee?' she asked.

'Better not.' He moved his head very slightly in the direction of the photographer who was loitering in view of the door to her flat, reminding her that they were being watched.

It was a good thing, in a way, she thought. The smell of coffee really made her feel sick. But she missed the old days when Dragan would have carried her up the stairs to her bed. Or to his.

'Dragan…' She stopped. No, now wasn't the time or the place.

'What?'

'Nothing. Just I'm sorry I'm not good company tonight.'

'Still not heard from Serena?' he asked softly.

'Yes. But there's nothing to tell. *Papà* seems OK with the

idea of finding an alternative solution, but *Mamma...*'
Melinda shook her head in exasperation.

Dragan smiled. 'Could this be where you get your stubbornness?'

'Very funny. I'm nothing like her.' But she smiled back. 'So do I get a kiss goodnight?'

'"Just good friends" don't kiss each other goodnight,' he reminded her softly. 'And we've already talked long enough for that photographer to get very interested. He's just moved a bit closer.'

An added pressure on their relationship she could well do without. She sighed. 'Goodnight, then.'

'Goodnight.'

He waited while she unlocked the door, then smiled at her. 'Get some sleep. You'll feel better tomorrow.'

True. Once she had a date for her scan. And once she'd had the scan itself, it would be even better. 'I have a day off tomorrow.'

'Sleep in. It'll do you good,' he advised. 'I'll call you in the morning.'

Melinda had just stepped out of the shower the following morning when the phone shrilled.

She wrapped a towel around herself and hurried to answer it. Dragan? Or was it Chloe, with the news of the appointment? 'Hello?'

'Melinda, just *what* is all this about?' Viviana asked crisply.

Melinda grimaced when she heard her mother's voice. She really wasn't in the mood for another fight. 'Serena's already told you. We worked it out between us.'

'I don't mean that. The *headlines*, child,' Viviana said impatiently.

'What headlines?'

'You know very well which ones.'

'*Mamma*, I haven't seen a newspaper this morning.'

'How long have you known that you are pregnant?' her mother snapped.

'I…' Melinda was suddenly, horribly awake, as if someone had thrown a bucket of icy-cold water over her. 'Pregnant?'

'Unless the headlines are untrue, in which case we will be suing for libel.'

'But…' Melinda dragged in a breath. 'I don't understand how they could possibly know. I only found out myself the day before yesterday.'

'So you *are* pregnant? How *could* you be so stupid?' Viviana demanded.

Melinda put a protective hand on her abdomen. So much for Viviana being a delighted grandmother.

'Unmarried and pregnant by a Croatian refugee!' Viviana made an exclamation of contempt. 'Well, you have your wish. We cannot *possibly* crown you queen of Contarini now. Even if you get rid of the baby, the scandal will stick to you and damage the monarchy. I thought Raffi was the reckless one, but you—you have gone even further!'

No 'How are you feeling?', Melinda thought. No 'When's the baby due?'. No 'How's the morning sickness?'. No interest in anything except the wretched monarchy.

Exactly the same way it had been for her entire life.

'As far as we are concerned,' Viviana said, 'you are no longer our daughter.'

Melinda blinked. Had she just heard that right? 'You're dis-owning me?'

'Given how little loyalty you have shown to us, why do you sound so surprised?' Viviana said scornfully. 'You are no longer part of our family. And I wish you well with your Croatian *refugee*.' She spat the word as if it were an insult. And then she hung up.

Melinda stared at the phone in disbelief.

Her family had just disowned her.

And then something really horrible occurred to her.

If her mother had seen the papers… She had to reach Dragan before he saw them. She had to tell him the news before the paparazzi scooped her.

She glanced at the clock. Half past eight. Would he still be at home? Please, please don't let him have left for the surgery yet. She called his mobile.

'The mobile phone you are calling is switched off. Please leave a message or send a text.'

She couldn't tell him the news by voicemail! 'Dragan? It's Melinda. If you pick this up before I speak to you, please ring me urgently. I need to talk to you. It's really, really important.' She hung up and tried the surgery number.

Engaged.

As it always was at this time on a Monday—the rush time after the weekend, when people who'd been feeling rough over the weekend rang to get an appointment to see the doctor.

Well, she'd redial as many times as she had to until she got through.

And she'd have to hope that she caught him before his first appointment.

The waiting room was practically silent.

This definitely wasn't normal, Dragan thought. People usually chatted to each other; Penhally was a warm, friendly place, and the surgery here wasn't the inner city waiting rooms full of silent strangers avoiding each other's eyes.

'What's happened?' he asked.

'Nothing,' Hazel mumbled, but she wouldn't look him in the eye.

'Have the press been harassing you again?'

She shook her head.

He glanced round at the waiting room; people shuffled in

their seats and looked away. But the second he looked back at Hazel, he was aware of people staring at him. 'Why is everyone staring at me?' he asked softly.

She looked really embarrassed, and handed him the newspaper in silence.

The headline on the front page screamed at him: THE DOCTOR'S ROYAL LOVE-CHILD

And suddenly he couldn't breathe.

It took a huge effort and every bit of concentration he possessed to walk into his consulting room. He stared at the page and read it over and over again, but he couldn't take the words in.

Melinda was pregnant.

With his child.

And once again the press knew all about it before he did.

Why the hell hadn't she told him?

So much for her promise of no more secrets.

She'd lied to him yet again.

Or was this some elaborate bluff, some excuse to get her out of being the queen of Contarini?

Or—even worse—had she planned the whole thing? Was this why she'd asked him to make love to her without protection the night before she'd gone away, knowing what her family would ask of her? She'd been so emphatic about it being her safe time. Had it been yet another layer of lies? Had she deliberately tried to get pregnant by a man she knew her family would never accept?

Feeling used and angry—and convinced now that Melinda had never really loved him at all—he picked up his mobile phone and speed-dialled her number.

It was engaged.

Great. Just great. His world had been turned upside down and shaken like a child's snowglobe, and he couldn't even talk to her about it.

To hell with the paparazzi and playing nice. He wanted answers. If he had to kick her door down to get them, he damned well would. Grimly, he keyed in a short message—a message he knew would get a reaction—and sent it to her mobile phone.

He flicked the intercom to let Hazel know he was ready for his first patient.

And then, after surgery, he'd have it out with Melinda.

CHAPTER TWELVE

'I'M SORRY, Melinda, he's with a patient,' Hazel informed her. 'Oh, and congratulations, by the way.'

Oh, no.

Oh, no, no, *no*.

If Hazel knew, that meant everyone in the surgery knew.

Including Dragan.

She was way, way too late.

And he was going to be so hurt and angry because he was the last one to know. After she'd promised him no more secrets, too—just to rub salt into his wounds.

But how on earth had the paparazzi found out?

'Thank you,' she muttered. 'Um, could you tell him I called?'

'Of course, love. And I've got this lovely pattern for a little matinee jacket—I'll knit you some in lemon and white. Because we don't know if you're having a girl or a boy yet, do we?'

'Thank you, Hazel. That's very kind.' It was a real effort to chat and be nice when all she wanted to do right now was get off the phone.

Her mobile phone beeped, telling her that someone had sent her a text.

'Um, Hazel, I won't hold you up because I know how busy the surgery is on a Monday morning,' she said quickly.

'Well, I'm sure I'll see you soon, dear,' Hazel said.

With relief, Melinda said goodbye, hung up and switched to the message.

New message from Dragan flashed onto the screen.

She flicked into the message. It was very short and to the point. *No more secrets?*

Even though a text message was just words and it was impossible to tell the sender's tone, she knew from his choice of words that he was absolutely livid. And she couldn't blame him: this was news he should have heard from her and nobody else.

He'd be hurt, too. Because she'd let him down. She'd promised him no more secrets—and then this had happened.

But she'd tried to get hold of him. Hadn't he heard her message?

Maybe his voicemail was having problems. She'd text him instead. And Hazel was bound to tell him that she'd phoned, so he would at least know she'd tried to get hold of him.

Sorry, not meant to be like this. We need to talk. Please call me.

She had no idea when he'd pick up the message. Maybe during his break or at the end of surgery—and despite the fact that consultations were only supposed to take ten minutes, Dragan never rushed his patients. Sometimes his surgery overran slightly, cutting into his lunch-break, and he'd been known to fit in extra patients, too, not wanting them to have to wait until the next surgery.

Wait.

Ha.

All she could do right now was *wait*.

She didn't dare venture outside. Given that the press had the news of her pregnancy, the place was probably crawling with paparazzi, and she really didn't feel up to answering questions. But there was another call she had to make.

She rang the surgery. 'Hi, Rachel, it's Melinda. Is George around?'

'He's just finishing with a patient. Want me to grab him before his next appointment and get him to ring you?' the receptionist asked.

'Yes, please. Is, um, is everything OK down there?'

'We had a few people in but George got rid of them,' Rachel said. 'Are *you* all right, Melinda?'

No. Far from it. 'Yes,' she lied.

Five minutes later, George called her back. 'This is getting to be a bit of a habit,' she said wryly. 'And I apologise. I take it you've seen the papers today?'

'Yes.'

'Things are a bit messy,' she said.

He laughed. 'We've got siege conditions outside. I hope you've got your blackout curtains up.'

'George, I would've told you. But I only found out myself two days ago. I don't even know when the baby's due. I'm waiting for my ultrasound appointment.'

'It's all right,' he reassured her. 'Legally, you don't have to tell me yet anyway. But I'm glad I do know, because I need to make sure your job conditions are suitable.'

'I'm a vet, George. And the surgery's just had a refit.'

'Not *those* sorts of conditions. In our profession, you know as well as I do there are cases you need to avoid during pregnancy on health and safety grounds. So there are some rules, and they're not breakable under any circumstances. Number one, you don't go anywhere near lambs; number two, you're meticulous about hygiene; and, number three, you wear gloves if you go anywhere near a cat. Understood?'

'I know. Because of the risks of chlamydophilia, listeria and toxicarosis.' Organisms that could all be harmful to unborn babies—and to their mothers.

'Exactly. You don't take any risks. You don't take any of my calls to large animals. And if there's a heavy animal in the surgery that needs to be up on the table, you get help—you *don't* do the lifting yourself. Got it?'

'Got it,' she said.

'Good. Now, try and get some rest today. Everyone in the practice is under instructions to say "No comment" to just about anything. But if you need anything, you just tell us. Rachel can nip out to the shops for you if you need something and she can bring it in to you through the back.'

'George, you're a wonderful man and I don't deserve you as a boss. I owe you your body weight in chocolate,' she said feelingly.

'I might just take you up on that,' he teased. 'Still, at least your other half's a doctor. He'll keep a good eye on you.'

'Mmm.' Though right now she wasn't too sure Dragan was still her other half. Far from the baby drawing them closer together, overcoming the last hurdles between them, the news could be the thing to shatter their relationship for good.

She waited all morning. And finally, at lunchtime, Dragan called her. His voice was like ice when he said, 'It isn't very nice discovering through the newspapers that you're going to be a father.'

'I'm sorry. It wasn't supposed to happen that way.' She hadn't even begun to think how she'd tell him, but she'd never intended him to find out like this. She sighed. 'Look, I really don't want to talk about this over the phone. Can I see you?'

'With all the paparazzi swarming round? The surgery's besieged.'

'It's bad here, too.'

'I doubt if we can both give them the slip. So it's the phone or risking more speculation. Your choice.'

'Believe me, *you* won't be the one in the news tomorrow,' she said dryly. 'That will be me. And then, as an ex-princess, I'll cease to be news and they'll go away.'

'Ex-princess? What do you mean, ex-princess?'

'I'll explain when I see you.' She swallowed hard. 'So do I come over to you or are you coming here?'

'I'll come over.'

The few minutes it took to walk from the surgery to the vet's felt like hours. Cars were parked everywhere—including on the double yellow lines—and people were shouting at him.

'Congratulations, Dr Love-ak!'

Lord, how he hated the way they'd mangled his name for the headlines.

'How does it feel to be a soon-to-be dad?'

How the hell should he know? He hadn't really had time to take it in.

'Are you going to be king of Contarini?'

Absolutely *not*.

'Give us a smile!'

Yeah, right.

He resolutely ignored them. And he wasn't leading them to Melinda's back door either; he walked through the front door into the vet's.

'Dr Lovak!' Rachel looked up from the reception desk at him, surprised. 'I didn't think Bramb— Oh.' Her voice tailed off as she realised that, for once, the dog wasn't with him.

At least there were no paparazzi here; he knew everyone in the waiting room. Though the sympathetic smiles mixed with speculative looks made him uncomfortable. He lowered his voice. 'Can I nip through the back way to Melinda's? I want to avoid the posse outside.' He raised an eyebrow. 'How did you manage to keep them out?'

'George told them the next person to step inside was the one who'd help him sort out the next gelding, with no anaesthetic—and he'd be standing between the stallion's back legs, holding the relevant bits.'

Despite his anger, Dragan couldn't help smiling back at her. 'George has quite a way with words.' Not to mention that he was the same height as Dragan and much broader in the shoulders—if he drew himself up to his full height he could look very intimidating. 'Maybe I should take a leaf out of his book. I could borrow an epidural kit from Kate and threaten them with the syringe.'

'Ah, but then they'd have your picture all over the front page, captioned "Doctor Doom" or something like that,' Rachel said.

'Which might be marginally better than Dr *Love*-ak.' He grimaced. 'Thanks, Rachel.'

He went through the back of the surgery to the lobby, which also contained the door to Melinda's flat, and knocked on the door.

When she answered, he could see how pale and unhappy she looked—and although his first instinct was to wrap her in his arms and hold her close and tell her everything would be all right, he held back.

Because he was extremely angry with her. For keeping this from him. For letting him find out something important through the press yet again. What else had she kept from him? All the secrets and lies... He didn't want a life based on that, and he was beginning to realise that that was exactly what he'd get with Melinda. A life of subterfuge. Of keeping the stiff upper lip she'd once teased him of developing. And he really, really didn't want that. He didn't want their love for each other chipped away until he began to resent her and she started to despise him.

Without comment, Melinda stood aside and beckoned him in. She closed the door and followed him up the stairs.

Ah, hell.

Last time he'd been in this flat with her, he'd made love with her. Had that been the night they'd made the baby?

He clenched his fists. Why had it all had to go so wrong? Why did life have to be so bloody complicated?

'So when were you going to tell me?' he asked.

'I only found out myself on Saturday afternoon.'

'You saw me last night. Why didn't you tell me then?'

'Because I don't know how pregnant I am. I wanted to wait until I knew the due date.'

He shook his head. 'I don't understand. No more secrets, you said. So how come the press knew?'

'I have no ide—' Her voice faded, and he could see the worry on her face.

'What?' he asked suspiciously.

'Chloe wouldn't have said a word. So they must have gone through my bin and found the test kit or the packaging. *Dio.* I can't believe I was so stupid. What was I thinking?'

It took a moment for her comment to penetrate his brain. 'Hang on. *Chloe* knows? You told *Chloe* before you told *me*?'

'I needed professional advice,' Melinda defended herself. 'And apart from being a midwife, she's one of my best friends.'

'Don't you think that the baby's father should have been the first to know?'

'What was I supposed to tell you? I'm pregnant but I have no idea *how* pregnant?'

'I'm a GP, for pity's sake.' He stared at her. 'Don't you think *I* could've helped you?'

'I'm not your patient—and it's not ethical for you to treat me.'

'*You're* pulling me up on ethics?'

'I didn't mean it like that! I'm sorry.' She raked a hand through her hair. 'Look, I needed time to get used to the idea before I told you.'

Being pregnant was a huge life change, and of course she needed time to get used to the idea. And if she hadn't been Princess Melinda, it wouldn't have mattered. She would have had that time, and it wouldn't have been spread all over the press before she was ready to talk to him.

Though he was still hurt that she'd told Chloe first. And there was the issue with the scan: she was pregnant with their baby, and she hadn't asked him to go to the dating scan with her, as any normal man would want to do. It felt as if she'd pushed him out—that they were making a new family between them and she'd cut him off before he had a chance to be part of it.

'So what are you planning to do? About the baby, I mean?' When she didn't answer immediately, he continued, 'That is, I assume there really *is* a baby? It's not just a way of forcing your parents' hand?'

He regretted the question the second he'd asked it, because her face lost all colour.

'I can't believe you just said that.' Her voice was a cracked whisper.

'There have been so many secrets and lies flying about, I don't know what's true and what's not any more.'

She swallowed hard. 'I'm pregnant, Dragan. I did the test twice. Just to be sure. But I don't know when the baby's due—Chloe thinks I might be as much as three months already.' A muscle twitched in the side of her cheek. 'She's got me an ultrasound appointment for next week. She's coming with me.'

'It didn't occur to you that *I* might want to go with you?'

'For pity's sake, Dragan. You've kept me practically at arm's length since I came back from Contarini. I didn't know what to think, how you'd react. We never talked about having kids—I don't know whether being a dad is going to bring back all the memories of your family and make you unhappy, or whether you're pleased, or what.'

'So you're blaming me?'

'No, of course I'm not! I'm trying to work out what's in

your head, and failing miserably.' She groaned. 'This is all going hideously, hideously wrong.'

'It's not very nice from this side of the fence either.'

'No? Well, you try being pregnant and completely on your own.' She glared at him. 'Not only does my baby's father doubt every single word I say, my family have disowned me.'

He remembered what she'd said about being an ex-princess. 'What do you mean, they've disowned you?'

'My mother saw the papers this morning. So that's how I found out the press knew. She rang me when I was in the shower. And as from this morning I'm no longer part of the Contarini royal family,' she said dryly.

'I suppose that solves one of your problems, then. If you're no longer Princess Melinda, they can't make you rule Contarini.'

She stared at him. 'Are you suggesting I did this *deliberately*?'

Had she? Right now, he really didn't know. He didn't have a clue what was going on in her head. 'I remember a certain night when you talked me out of using a condom.'

Melinda flinched. 'Apart from the fact I'm almost certainly more than a couple of weeks pregnant... If you can believe that of me, then I suggest you leave. Right now. Because I'd rather bring up our child on my own than be with someone who has such a low opinion of me.'

Memories of his family flashed before his eyes. How his older brother had planned to marry his childhood sweetheart. The way his parents had talked about having grandchildren, reliving their memories of their own children with such happiness. The nursery furniture his brother and father were going to build together. His own role in the family as best man and godfather and uncle.

All gone, because his brother had died before the wedding could take place.

And now Melinda was putting a barrier between him and their child. He'd lost his new family before it had even begun.

'I can't deal with this,' Dragan said, and walked out. Before the bitterness in his throat choked him.

CHAPTER THIRTEEN

MELINDA spent the next few days as if she were in a trance. As she'd expected, the headlines were screaming about the royal vet being kicked out of the monarchy. But that would die down soon enough—at least now she had one less problem to deal with.

The only saving grace of that particular mess had been the call from her younger sister. 'Lini? It's me. I've just seen the papers and I could murder our mother! I've told her that, whatever happens, I still love you and you will always be my sister. And I've also told *Mamma* exactly what I think of her behaviour.' Serena's tone was caustic. 'She wanted to know if you'd taught me the swear words I used.'

'Oh, no.'

Serena laughed. 'I told her that I'd been the one to teach them to Raffi, actually, and she went off to get the smelling salts, muttering about how disgraceful my generation is. She's going to be in for a shock when *Papà* hands over to me, because I'm dragging Contarini into the twenty-first century, whether it likes it or not.' She paused. 'Well, I'm looking forward to being an auntie. And to meeting your Dragan properly.'

Melinda swallowed hard. 'You've seen the papers. I don't think he is my Dragan any more.'

'Don't be silly. Of course he is. I remember everything that you told me while you were over here. It's obvious that you love him and he loves you.'

'It's not as simple as that.'

'Everything's simple,' Serena said crisply. 'People just think too hard and then they complicate things. He loves you and you love him. You're expecting his baby. The only thing that was standing in your way was the monarchy. And now that hurdle's gone, there's no reason for you not to be together.'

'He walked out on me, Rena.'

'So you had a fight. Patch it up. Don't be too proud about it,' Serena counselled softly. 'Go and see him. Tell him how you really feel about him.'

'Maybe.'

'Stop messing about and just *do* it.'

'Hey, you're not queen yet. You can't order me around,' Melinda said, trying to keep it light.

'I can try.' Serena's voice grew serious. 'Lini, I meant what I said. Just forget what *Mamma* said. It's not true. You'll always be my sister. And I'll always be there for you—just as you've always been there for me. If it wasn't for you, I'd never be able to do this job, because you're the one who's shown me I can do anything if I try. Look at you—you left home at eighteen and went to study in a foreign country. And veterinary science is hard enough in Italian, let alone in a different language. So you showed me how to reach for the stars—how something might seem impossible but I could do it if I tried hard enough.'

'I really am going to cry now.'

'Don't. Call Dragan and tell him you love him. And when you get the first picture from the scan, if you don't send me a copy right away I'll have you chucked in the palace dungeons.'

'Noted, Your Highness,' Melinda said.

Serena just laughed. 'Don't think I don't mean it. Look, I have to go, *cara*. But you call me if you need me, OK?'

'I will. And thank you, Rena. I thought...' Melinda choked back the words.

'You think too much. Now go and do as your sovereign-to-be orders.'

But Dragan wasn't answering his phone. Melinda assumed that he was out somewhere with Bramble. But the longer she left it, the harder it was to make the call, until she didn't make it at all.

Work kept her busy the next day.

And then she had a callout to the caravan park. There had been a dogfight, and one of the animals had been badly bitten. 'I know I should've told them to bring the dog down here,' Rachel said, 'but the girl was hysterical.'

'OK. I can always bring the dog back myself, if need be,' Melinda said.

But when she pulled in to the caravan park, she recognised one of the other cars in the car park. Dragan's. Rachel could have warned her that a doctor had been called out, too.

Well, Penhally wasn't that big a place. She'd have to face him some time. May as well be now. She lifted her chin, straightened her spine and went over to where he was treating a teenage boy whose arm was bloodstained. Next to him, a girl was on her knees beside an elderly Yorkshire terrier lying on a picnic blanket, stroking its head and crying her eyes out.

Dragan looked at her, unsmiling.

She might not want to talk to him on a personal level, but she'd show him she could be professional. 'Dr Lovak,' she said, giving him a cool nod of acknowledgement.

'Ms Fortescue,' he responded.

'I'm Melinda, the vet,' she said to the girl. 'You're Colleen, who rang about your dog?'

The girl nodded. 'My mum's going to *kill* me,' she quavered.

'What happened?'

'I was taking Bruiser for a walk. Except I wasn't looking after him properly.' She flushed. 'I was talking to Micky.'

Micky being the boy with the bloody arm. Clearly a holiday romance, Melinda thought with a pang. One that the poor girl would remember for all the wrong reasons.

Without meaning to, she caught Dragan's eye. And she could see from his expression that he was thinking exactly the same thing.

It was a mess.

Just like their relationship.

'And this dog came out of nowhere,' Micky said. 'It attacked Bruiser. And when I tried to get it off him it bit me, too.'

'Micky was so brave.' Colleen sniffed.

'Where's the other dog now?' Melinda asked.

'The police have got it,' Micky said. 'It ought to be put down.'

'Make sure the police have your details—and that they've made a note on the Dog Bite Register. That way, if that dog routinely attacks other dogs, they can do something about it. Now, let me have a look at Bruiser here.' She dropped to her knees and let the dog sniff her hands for reassurance that she wasn't going to hurt him, then gently examined the dog. 'There's one pretty nasty bite here. Are all his vaccinations up to date, Colleen?'

The girl nodded.

'That's one good thing. How old is he?'

'Nine. We got him when I was six.'

'OK.' Gently, she cleaned the wounds, talking to the dog and reassuring him as she did so—just as Dragan was irrigating the boy's wounds. Again, she couldn't help glancing at him, and discovered him looking straight at her, his expression unreadable.

He looked away first. 'I'm going to need to take you back to the surgery, Micky,' Dragan said. 'I need to give you some antibiotics, just to make sure there was nothing nasty in the dog's bite.'

'I'm going to need to give Bruiser antibiotics, too,' Melinda said. 'And I'm not going to stitch the wounds closed because there's more of a risk of infection with puncture wounds.'

'Same with you, Micky,' Dragan said. 'I'm going to cover your wounds with a light dressing, and you'll need to come back to me in a couple of days for stitches.'

'Snap,' Melinda said to Colleen with a smile.

'Is Bruiser going to be all right?' she asked. 'He's not going to die?'

'He's going to be a bit sore for a few days. And you need to keep an eye on him—if you notice anything unusual about his breathing or if he seems hot or uncomfortable, call me straight away.' She gave the girl one of the practice business cards. 'So where's your mum?'

'She's gone shopping in the village.'

'OK. When she gets back, ask her to ring me and I'll explain. It wasn't your fault that Bruiser was attacked. If she'd been with you, it would still have happened,' Melinda reassured the girl.

'You probably saved the dog's life,' Dragan told Micky. 'Though next time you might find a bucket of water's more effective and less painful for you in breaking up a fight. Better let your parents know where you're going—I'll drop you back here when I've sorted the antibiotics.'

'Are you all right?' Melinda asked Colleen.

The girl nodded and continued to stroke the dog. 'I'm just so sorry he got hurt.'

Yeah. Melinda knew how that felt. Again, she glanced at Dragan—and met his unfathomable dark gaze.

'It'll work out,' she said to Colleen.

Though she was none too sure if the situation between her and Dragan could be fixed. They'd worked as a team here, sorting out a problem. He was a brilliant doctor and she knew she was good at her job, too. They were both good at reassuring others. So why couldn't they reassure themselves?

She had no idea where they went from here. All she knew was that she missed him. And she had to find a way to get through to him, to prove to him that she loved him and she'd never hurt him again.

Later that evening George rang her, sounding anxious. 'Melinda? When's your dating scan again?'

'Wednesday afternoon.'

'And you're not sure just how pregnant you are.'

Ice trickled down her spine. There had to be a reason why he was asking. And from the tone of his voice, it was a serious reason. 'Why?'

'You know when you helped me at Polkerris Farm when lambing went mad a few weeks back?'

'Ye-es.' Usually Melinda dealt with the small-animal work at the practice, but that particular week there had been more lambs than George could deal with on his own, and she'd gone over to the farm to help him out.

'I asked you before we started if there was any possibility you were pregnant, and you said no.'

'I didn't think I was.'

George dragged in a breath. 'Then you need to see your midwife and ask her to do some tests.'

Melinda's mouth felt almost too stiff to move. 'You're telling me that some of the ewes are losing their lambs?'

'It's definitely EAE.' EAE stood for enzootic abortion in ewes, and it was every sheep farmer's worst nightmare at lambing time. The infection could also be transferred to humans, so pregnant women were advised to avoid all contact with lambs, ewes who were lambing and even the boots and clothes of people who'd been involved in lambing.

'I'm taking samples,' George said. He paused. 'Look, is there anyone who can be with you?'

Dragan.

No. Not after this afternoon. His coldness had made his feelings clear. 'I'll ring Chloe.'

'Do that. And actually she's probably the best person to give you advice. Let me know how things go—and if there's anything you need, you only have to say, OK?'

'I will. Thank you, George.'

Melinda cut the connection and pressed the speed-dial button for Chloe's number. Please, be there, she begged silently. Please be there.

The phone rang.

And rang.

And rang.

By the time it was finally picked up, Melinda was frantic. 'Chloe? It's Melinda. Can I come over? Please?'

'Melinda?'

What was Dragan doing at Chloe's place? And why was he answering her phone?

She must have asked the questions out loud because he said, 'You didn't call Chloe. You called *me*.'

It must've been her subconscious dialling the wrong number. Because when George had broken the news, she'd wanted Dragan with her so badly.

'What's wrong?' he asked.

She'd tried so hard to be strong. But hearing him sound so warm, so concerned—the way he used to be—was too much for her. She couldn't handle this, not when they weren't together any more. The weight of all that had happened suddenly hit her. She dropped the phone and sobbed.

Three minutes later her doorbell rang. As if someone was leaning on it. Hard. And it didn't stop ringing until she stumbled down the stairs and opened the door.

He closed the door behind him and wrapped his arms round her. 'It's all right. Calm down. Deep breaths. It's OK.'

Sobs racked her.

'Is it the baby?' he asked.

'N-no. Y-yes.' She couldn't get the words out.

'Are you bleeding?'

'N-no. It's…it's…'

'All right, *carissima*. I'm here. I've got you.' And he lifted her bodily, cradling her against him with one hand under her knees and the other supporting her back.

Just as if he were carrying her over the threshold.

Which wasn't going to happen.

She shivered, even more miserable now—wanting him to go away and yet wanting him close at the same time.

This was all such a mess.

And if she lost the baby…

He gently placed her on the sofa and disappeared for a couple of moments, returning with a glass of water. 'Here. Small sips. Slowly.' When her breathing had slowed, he stroked her face. 'Now tell me what's wrong.'

She dragged in a breath. 'I've been exposed to EAE.'

He frowned. 'I thought you only did the small-animals side?'

'I do. But George was run ragged, so I helped him out on Polkerris Farm. He just called to tell me…' She shuddered. 'He says the flock's got EAE.'

'And when was this that you helped out?'

'A few weeks back. There wasn't any sign of it then.' She shook her head. 'And George asked me if I was pregnant before I started helping. I said no—because I didn't think I was. I swear I had no idea. I would never, ever risk our baby like that.'

'I know you wouldn't.' He held her close. 'First we need to take a blood sample for testing. Has Chloe booked you in yet, done the usual tests?'

'No. We were going to do that just before the scan.'

'Right. Well, we can sort that out now. And we need to find out just how pregnant you are. Right now I'd say try not to panic because there's a very good chance everything's going to be fine.' He shifted her very slightly so he could retrieve his mobile phone from his pocket, then dialled a number and waited. 'Maternity department, please.'

Clearly he was ringing St Piran Hospital.

'Hello? It's Dr Dragan Lovak from Penhally. I have a pregnant mum who's been exposed to EAE, but we're not sure of her dates. Yes, a few weeks back. No, no bloods or scans yet. That's great. Forty minutes? That'd be perfect. Thank you so much. Yes. Her name's Melinda Fortesque. Thank you.' He cut the connection and looked at Melinda. 'They're going to give you a scan to check your dates, and do the blood test. It's a half-hour drive from here to St Piran, so you've got time to wash your face if you want.' Then he went all inscrutable on her. 'Would you rather someone else took you? Shall I call Chloe?'

'No.' She wanted him. Though right now she didn't want to move: she was in his arms, just where she belonged.

'All right. Wash your face while I go and get my car.'

'What about the press?'

Dragan said something in Croatian that she couldn't translate but she was pretty sure it was extremely rude. 'You're more important,' he said.

She dragged in a breath. 'Thank you. It's more than I deserve after the way I've treated you.' Yes, he'd walked out on her, but she'd told him to leave. And she'd kept him in the dark about too many things.

He made no comment.

'We can take my car, if it would save time.'

'OK—but I'll drive,' he said, 'because you're really not in a fit state.'

She didn't argue. And she washed her face and cleaned her teeth, then managed to keep herself together while they got to the car.

To her relief, no paparazzi were around. Or, if they were, they kept well hidden.

'So how can they tell if I've been affected by the lambing?'

'They'll do a blood test,' Dragan explained. 'It's what they call complement fixation testing, but that on its own won't tell them if you've been exposed to an ovine strain or an avian strain. They'll do immunofluorescent testing to sort that out.' He looked grim. 'Have you had any flu-like symptoms?'

'No.'

'That's good.'

'Is it?' She remembered the leaflets she'd read. 'I thought it was asymptomatic in humans.'

'It can be,' he admitted.

'How's it treated?'

'Antibiotics—usually a two-week course of erythromycin.'

She frowned. 'But aren't antibiotics bad during pregnancy?'

'Let's not cross that bridge just yet. We don't know you've definitely been infected and we don't know how pregnant you are.' He took his left hand off the wheel for a moment to hold hers. 'If it helps, most reported cases of problems are in the period from twenty-four to thirty-six weeks, and I'm pretty sure your dates aren't in that area. And it's also very, very rare for someone to lose a baby because of it nowadays.'

'Because everyone knows the guidelines. If you're a vet or you work with sheep, and someone in your family's pregnant, you stay away from them during lambing—you don't even let them near your clothes or boots, because they can pick it up from there. And it can cause problems with the baby's development. I've seen the leaflets and the advisory notes, Dragan. I know what it can do. And I know what it can do to me, too. DIC.'

'Disseminated intravascular coagulation is an extremely rare complication.'

'But it's a possibility.' One which could kill her, if the heavy bleeding went along with shock and infection. She'd once heard Chloe talk about it and it had shocked her that in this century women could still die in childbirth. 'So are complications of the liver and the kidneys. And EAE can lead to a woman losing the baby.'

'In the severe form of the disease. And the chances are very high that you don't have that.'

'But what if I do? What if I've got it and I don't have the symptoms?' She dragged in a breath. 'I didn't know I was pregnant when I went out to the farm. I swear I didn't.'

'Nobody's blaming you, *carissima*. And it's going to be all right.'

'Is it? You can't give me a guarantee, can you?' She released his hand and wrapped her arms round her abdomen. 'I can't lose this baby, I can't.' Her breath came out in a shudder. 'It's all I have left of you.'

As the words penetrated his brain, Dragan was stunned.

Melinda was so upset that clearly she was speaking from the heart instead of playing a role.

And what she'd just said…

It's all I have left of you.

She wanted the baby because it was *his*, not to get her out of being queen of Contarini.

So these past few days of hell, when he'd thought she'd used him and had never really loved him—he'd been completely wrong. Paranoid, stupid and just plain wrong.

Because Melinda loved him.

She really, really loved him.

And she wanted this baby because it was his.

Right now she was vulnerable. Her real self, not hiding. And she needed him to be strong for her. Needed him. Wanted *him*. After all, when she'd thought she'd been calling Chloe, she'd rung *his* number. He was the one she'd needed.

He swallowed hard. 'You're not going to lose our baby.' He hoped to hell she wasn't. It all depended on whether she'd been infected by the bacterium and what stage the pregnancy was. 'And you haven't lost me either. I'm sorry. You gave me a hard time—but I've given you a hard time, too. We're as bad as each other.'

'I never meant to hurt you.'

'And I never meant to hurt you.'

Again, he reached across to hold her hand. Her hand gripped his so tightly, she was close to cutting off his circulation, but he didn't care. And he was glad that they were on a straight bit of road right now with no roundabouts or traffic lights ahead—because he would really, really resent having to loosen her hand to change gear.

'It's going to be all right,' he promised softly. 'And I'm going to be there with you every single step of the way.'

They made it to the hospital with five minutes to spare. Just enough time to get to the maternity department—and Dragan kept his arm round Melinda the whole time.

It was the first time she'd felt warm since her return to England.

Until they reached the maternity ward and Melinda saw the whiteboard with her name on it, in the column marked EMERGENCY. '*Porca miseria!*' She clapped a hand to her mouth, sounding horrified.

'It's written up there because they're expecting you in and I asked for an emergency scan,' Dragan said quietly. 'All it means is that you didn't have a pre-booked routine appointment. There's nothing to worry about, *cara*. I promise.'

He led her over to the reception desk, where one of the midwives was busy writing notes. 'I've brought Melinda Fortesque for a scan and to see Mr Perron.'

The midwife looked up and smiled. 'Have a seat. I'll let him know you're here.'

The wait seemed endless. And Melinda was still shaking even as the consultant came over and introduced himself, then took them into a small treatment room.

'I understand you're a vet,' he said.

She nodded. 'I didn't know I was pregnant when I helped out with the lambing. It was a few weeks ago, and my boss tells me the farm's been hit by EAE. We don't know the cause yet, but as chlamydiosis is the most common…' Her voice faded.

'You've done the right thing in coming here,' Mr Perron said. 'I know it's hard, but try not to worry. It's pretty rare that women are affected by chlamydiosis, and even rarer that the baby's affected—there are fewer than ten cases a year nowadays.'

'Because people are aware of the risks.'

'Even so. Try not to worry,' he said gently. 'And this is your doctor?'

'Her partner,' Dragan corrected.

'Sorry.' The consultant checked the notes. 'Must be crossed wires. It's down here that you're her doctor.'

'I'm a GP, yes,' Dragan said, 'but not Melinda's. I just rang through to save time.'

Mr Perron nodded. 'So you know what we're going to do.'

'Blood test and an ultrasound to give us some dates,' Melinda said.

'We'll do the nasty bit first,' Mr Perron said. 'Can you make a fist for me, Ms Fortesque?'

'Melinda.'

'Melinda,' he said with a smile, checking for access to a vein in her inner elbow. 'Pump it for me… That's good. Now, sharp scratch…' She flinched, and he took the blood sample and then labelled it. 'The results won't be back for a couple of days, but do try not to worry. Have you had any flu-like symptoms at all?'

'Nothing. No chills or fever, no cough, no headache.'

'How about a sore throat or any joint pains?' Mr Perron asked. At her shake of the head he added, 'Any problems with bright light?'

'Nothing.'

'Sickness?'

Melinda dragged in a breath. 'Oh, *Dio*. I thought it was morning sickness. And it's only been this week.'

'Then it probably *is* morning sickness, and it affects women in very different ways,' he reassured her. 'There's no guarantee if you have morning sickness in one pregnancy you'll have it in the next—and vice versa. Now, let's have a look at the scan. Can you get onto the couch for me and bare your tummy?'

She did so, and Dragan sat next to her, holding her hand tightly.

'I'm going to put some gel on your stomach—I'm afraid this is the portable scanner so the gel's going to feel cold. The gel's always warmer in the ultrasound department than it is here.' He smiled at her. 'Right. Then I'm going to stroke this over your abdomen—you might feel a little bit of pressure, but it shouldn't hurt at all. Can you both see the screen?'

'Yes,' Dragan said.

'And… *Voilà*.'

Dragan gazed in wonder at the screen.

Their baby.

Two arms, two legs, a head. Definitely alive and kicking. And he could see the heart beating.

Mr Perron did some measurements. Without even needing to look at a chart, he smiled. 'I'd say from this you're about ten weeks.'

'And everything's all right?'

'Two arms, two legs, a head, a nicely beating heart.' He

moved the scanner round. 'Your placenta's in the right place, too, so nothing to worry about there.'

Dragan couldn't take his eyes off the screen. A little life. Something he and Melinda had created. The beginning of their family. His fingers tightened round hers.

'Could we…? Is it possible to have a picture, please?' Melinda asked.

Mr Perron shook his head regretfully. 'This is the portable scanner and it's not hooked up to a printer. I'm afraid you'll have to wait until your dating scan. Unless…' He paused. 'Do you have a mobile phone?'

'Yes, and I switched it off before we came into the hospital,' Dragan said.

'Does it have a camera?'

'Yes.'

Mr Perron spread his hands. 'Well, then. There's the solution.'

'But—I thought you weren't supposed to use mobile phones in hospitals? In case it interfered with the equipment?' Melinda asked.

'It really depends on the area. I'd stop anyone using one in Intensive Care, the special baby care unit or where there's a lot of equipment being used—places where there's a high risk of electromagnetic interference or where a ringtone might sound like an alarm tone on medical equipment and there's a chance it might be missed.' Mr Perron gave her a rueful smile. 'And I have to admit, it drives the staff crazy if phones are going off all over the place, disturbing patients' rest or drowning out a discussion about someone's health-care plan. But you're taking a photograph of your own scan so it's not breaching patient confidentiality—and you're far enough away from any other equipment that it's not going to hurt anyone. Go ahead.'

'Thank you,' Dragan said, pulled his phone from his pocket, switched it on and took a couple of photographs.

'I'll be in touch with the blood results,' the consultant said. 'I think the chances are that you'll be fine, but if there is a problem we can start treatment immediately.' He handed Dragan some paper towels.

Dragan cleaned the gel off Melinda's stomach and restored order to her clothes. When she sat up, he held her close.

'I'll give you a minute or two,' Mr Perron said softly. 'It's always emotional, the first time you see the baby on a scan.'

Melinda had no idea how long they stayed like that, just holding each other. But when they pulled apart and she looked at Dragan, she could see that his eyelashes were wet, too. The scan had moved him just as much as it had moved her.

'I've missed you so much,' she said. 'And I didn't do this on purpose, Dragan.'

'I know that now—and I'm sorry. I thought you were using me.'

She shook her head. 'I'd never do that. And besides, we didn't make the baby that night. It was long before then. I know we used condoms, but you know as well as I do that the only one hundred per cent reliable method of contraception is abstinence.' She looked at him. 'I wouldn't use you like that. I love you.'

He stroked her face. 'I love you, too. *Volim te.*'

'Do you?' She wasn't so sure. He'd walked away from her.

'Yes.' He brushed his mouth against hers. 'These last few days rank among the most miserable of my entire life. When I thought I'd lost you—and the baby—it felt as bad as when I lost my family.'

'So why did you walk out on me?'

'Pride. Stupidity, because I let my pride get in the way. I should've stayed to fight for you.'

'Me, too.'

'Let's go home,' he said softly.

'Home?'

'To hell with the papers. They can print what they like. You and the baby are the only ones who matter. Before you went back to Contarini, we were planning to move in together. Get married. So let's do it.'

'You still want to marry me?'

'I never stopped wanting to marry you,' he said softly. 'But I tried to do the right thing. To let you go back to Contarini so you weren't cut off from your family.'

'They chose to do that anyway.' She closed her eyes.

'We can sort it out. Because I'm on your side,' he reminded her.

'My mother—'

'Will be fine. She'll be reconciled with us. I have a plan.' He stroked her hair. 'Your official dating scan is…when?'

'Wednesday.'

'And your next time off is…?'

'The weekend after.'

'Mine, too,' he said. 'I'll book Bramble in with Lizzie and we'll fly over to Contarini. Pay your family a visit. I think it's time your mother discovered that family is more important than duty. And, faced with you and a certain photograph, I think she'll soften.'

Fear tricked down Melinda's spine. 'What if she doesn't?'

'She will. Trust me.'

'Because you're a doctor?'

He laughed. 'Or so the saying goes. *Sve ce biti okej.* Everything will be OK,' he translated. 'And we've got a wedding to plan. Last Saturday of April.'

Her eyes went wide. 'You what?'

'Unless you've talked to Reverend Kenner to call it all off, the wedding's booked for the last Saturday in April.' He smiled wryly. 'That's the one thing I didn't think to do. Speak to the vicar to say it wasn't going to happen any more. I suppose subconsciously I still hoped it would work out.'

'It's going to work out. Because I'm never, ever going to keep anything from you again.'

'No?'

'No.'

CHAPTER FOURTEEN

MELINDA'S booking-in appointment and scan went as planned. She'd just finished evening surgery on Wednesday when Chloe dropped into the vet's.

'I wanted to tell you in person,' she said with a smile. 'Mr Perron just rang your results through. You're clear.'

Melinda hugged her. 'Chloe—that's so…I…'

Chloe smiled. 'Hey, you're meant to start forgetting your words a bit later on in pregnancy than this!'

'I'm just so relieved—so happy.' Melinda hugged her again. 'You must come and celebrate with Dragan and me tonight.'

'No.' Chloe patted her arm. 'It's lovely of you to ask me, but this really should be just the two of you. At least you can relax and enjoy your pregnancy now.'

'Definitely.'

She locked up the surgery and walked with Chloe towards Fisherman's Row. 'Are you sure you won't come in?' she asked when they reached Dragan's door.

'I'm sure. This should be between just the two of you. Now, go and put him out of his misery. See you later.' Chloe walked further down to her house, while Melinda opened the door with the key Dragan had given her two days previously.

The key to his house.

Which he'd told her was now *their* house.

It might be small, but it was home—and she loved it here. Close to the sea, with a little patch of garden. And, best of all, Dragan was here.

Bramble bounded over to her, wagging her tail.

'Oh, you bad dog—you're supposed to be taking it easy, still, not leaping around,' Melinda scolded.

Bramble completely ignored the telling-off and licked her.

Dragan saved the file on his computer, then pushed his chair back and walked over to enfold her in his arms. 'Good day?' he asked.

'Better than good. Mr Perron just rang through to Chloe. We're in the clear.'

Dragan whooped, picked her up and twirled her round. 'That's fantastic. So now we can relax and just look forward to October.' He kissed her. 'I'm just so happy.'

'Me, too.'

They ended up celebrating in bed.

And the following evening they went late-night shopping in Newquay. For just one item. Melinda steered him away from the more expensive jeweller's shops.

'I can afford it, you know. The upside of living like a Spartan is that I have a fairly decent savings account,' Dragan said.

'I'd rather spend the money on the baby than on me.'

'There's enough for both of you.'

She sighed. 'I love you, Dragan, and I'd happily marry you with a plastic ring from a Christmas cracker. You don't have to make a fuss about precious metals and gemstones.'

Dragan laughed. 'I think we can do better than a plastic ring. Just have a look around. And we're not looking at prices—we're looking for something you *like*.'

He knew the second she'd seen the one because her eyes lit

up. A plain platinum band with an emerald-cut solitaire diamond.

And when she tried it on, it was a perfect fit.

'This was meant to be,' he said, bought it, and slipped the velvet-covered box into his pocket.

He considered giving her the ring over dinner, but it didn't feel right, getting officially engaged away from Penhally. The place that had brought them together.

'You know when I asked you to marry me, I said it should've been at sunrise?' he said conversationally when they were back in the village.

Melinda groaned. 'No. Please tell me you're not planning to make me get up before dawn tomorrow.'

'That was plan A,' he teased. 'But I'll settle for plan B. Bramble needs a walk. Coming?'

'I'm a little tired.'

'That was a rhetorical question,' he informed her. 'And we'll take it slowly.'

'Slow? With Bramble?' she teased. 'She's a husky in disguise!'

It was a clear evening, and the sky was full of stars. Better still, there were no paparazzi around as they strolled down the harbour towards the lighthouse. Everything was quiet; there was just the swish of the ocean as the waves lapped against the short.

'Lie down and wait,' Dragan told Bramble, who promptly did his bidding.

Then he turned to Melinda and dropped to one knee. 'Now I'm going to ask you properly. Melinda Fortesque, will you be my wife, my love, for the rest of our days?'

'Yes,' she whispered.

He took the ring from its box, slid it onto her finger, then stood up again, pulled her into his arms and kissed her. 'Thank you,' he said softly when he broke the kiss.

They strolled back home hand in hand, the dog trotting along beside them. As they passed the church, Dragan said, 'This is where we'll be, the last Saturday of the month.' He paused. 'Do we really have enough time to organise this wedding?'

'All we need is each other and a ring.'

He smiled. 'This is Penhally. Whether we like it or not, we're going to have a church full of friends. Even if we have the tiniest reception, we're going to have a huge wedding.' He looked at her. 'If it's too much for you, we can put it back a bit.'

Melinda shook her head. 'My sister Serena says that everything is simple until people complicate things.'

'Wise words,' Dragan said. 'Though we need to see your family before we can get married.'

'You don't have to ask my father's permission.'

'No, but I would like his blessing. Families are important, *cara*. And I want our marriage to start on the right note.'

'It will.' She squeezed his hand. 'And your family will be there in spirit. I hope they would have approved of me.'

Dragan had to swallow the lump in his throat. 'They would've *loved* you, Melinda. Just like I do.'

His family would have taken her straight to their hearts. But he had a feeling that her family wouldn't react to him in the same way. After all, she was a princess and he was just an ordinary man.

'That's something else I wanted to ask you, Dragan. The baby... If it's a boy, I'd like to name him after your father. And a girl after your mother.'

The lump in his throat grew even larger. 'Are you sure?'

She nodded.

'What about your parents? It's not fair to name a baby after one set of grandparents and not the other.'

Melinda smiled. 'That's one of the things I love about you, *carissimo*. Your sense of fairness. But I was thinking we'd have more than one baby...'

* * *

On Saturday morning Melinda and Dragan caught the early flight to London, then a connecting flight to Naples. The nearer they got to Italy, the quieter Melinda became. And Dragan noticed that she didn't talk at all during the flight to Contarini. He laced his fingers through hers.

'All right?' he asked softly.

'*Mi sento male*,' Melinda muttered. *I feel sick.*

His heart missed a beat. 'The baby?'

She shook her head. '*La mia famiglia*.'

So she was sick with nerves at facing her family? He noticed that she'd slipped back into her own tongue. He smiled reassuringly at her and squeezed her hand. '*Va bene, bella mia*. It will be all right.'

She sighed. 'I'm not so sure.'

'Your sister is on your side. And I am here. Trust me.'

Finally they landed. 'I booked a taxi. It was supposed to meet us here,' Melinda said when they'd gone through customs. She shook her head in annoyance. 'Maybe they're running late. I'll check.'

But before she could take her mobile phone out of her handbag, a woman sashayed towards them. She was slightly taller and thinner than Melinda, Dragan noticed, and her hair was worn back in a smooth Grace Kelly–type style rather than loose and wild, the way Melinda wore it—but the family resemblance was unmistakeable.

This had to be Melinda's younger sister.

'Did I hear someone asking for a taxi?' she said with a smile.

'Rena?' Melinda stared at her in obvious surprise. 'What are *you* doing here?'

'Meeting you, of course.'

'But—I had a taxi booked.'

'I know. I cancelled it. Carlo's outside.'

Melinda blinked. 'You brought the limo?'

'It makes life less complicated. Welcome home, *carissima*.'
The woman hugged her, then stood back and looked at Dragan.

He gave her a tiny formal bow. 'Your Royal Highness.'

She made a small impatient gesture and hugged him.
'Don't be so formal. You're going to be *mio cognato*, my
brother-in-law. So there's no need for any of this "Your Royal
Highness" business. My name is Serena. Or Rena, for short.'
She grinned. 'I must say, you're dishier than your photo-
graph.'

'Rena!' Melinda said, sounding shocked.

Serena laughed. 'And *you* look a million times happier than
the last time I saw you, Lini. Let me see the ring.' She held
Melinda's left hand and peered at the stone. 'Now, that's
pretty,' she said, her voice full of approval.

'Not quite in the league of your family jewels,' Dragan said
dryly.

'But this was given with love. Which makes it sparkle an
awful lot more,' Serena said, her voice utterly sincere.

He smiled at her. 'I think I'm going to like having a
sister-in-law.'

'Pity you have the demon mother-in-law to go with it,'
Serena said.

'Rena!' Melinda said again.

Serena laughed. 'I'm only saying what you're thinking,
sorella mia. Dragan versus the dragon…'

'Stop it. I'm worried enough about this.'

'Chill. It will be fine.' Serena gave an exaggerated wink.
'If *Mamma* misbehaves, the second I am queen I can chuck
her in the dungeons.'

'You'd never believe she was always the demure one, would
you?' Melinda asked Dragan as they followed Serena to the
limousine. 'This queen business is going right to her head.'

'The phrase, *sorella mia*, is "Off with her head",' Serena
corrected, laughing.

The journey was an easy one, and then Carlo drove through the gates to the palace. It was a huge mellow stone building, clearly several hundred years old. When they went inside, Dragan noted that the carpets were so thick he sank into them as he walked, and the curtains were of heavy velvet and brocade. Portraits hung close together on the walls: generation after generation of people who'd lived there.

Old money.

Breeding.

Tradition.

Royalty.

A million miles away from his little cottage in Penhally. This wasn't the kind of place where he belonged.

It wasn't where Melinda belonged either. And all of a sudden he began to understand how she'd felt on the plane. Because he was feeling exactly the same way right now—with adrenalin tingling through him.

Alessandro and Viviana were seated on couches in one of the formal rooms. And Dragan suddenly wished he'd thought to ask Melinda about etiquette. How did you behave around royalty? Both Melinda and Serena were down to earth and didn't stand on ceremony—but he knew their parents wouldn't be the same.

'*Mamma. Papà.*' Serena curtseyed before them both, and kissed both of them on the backs of their left hands.

Lord. He'd never, ever been anywhere so formal. Didn't these people greet their children with a hug and a kiss, like normal parents?

Then again, they weren't normal people. They were the king and queen of Contarini.

'*Mamma. Papà.*' Melinda also made a small curtsey, but there was no kiss.

And then all eyes were trained on him.

OK. He could do this. If Melinda and Serena had to

curtsey, it followed that he would have to bow. 'Your Majesties,' he said, first bowing to Melinda's father and then to her mother.

They nodded graciously.

And then it was the most awkward pause he'd ever experienced in his life.

'Be seated,' Viviana said, giving an imperious gesture towards one of the sofas.

No wonder Melinda had wanted to escape all this. It was *stifling*. Like going back in time a hundred and fifty years.

Alessandro looked at Dragan, his arms folded. 'So you are the man who wishes to ask for my permission to marry my daughter.'

What now? Was he supposed to say certain things in a certain way?

He didn't have a clue what the traditions were.

But the one thing he could do was to speak from his heart.

He stood up. 'Your Majesty, I love your daughter,' Dragan said quietly. 'She is the sunshine in my life. And I asked her to marry me before I found out she was a princess—before I discovered that she was expecting our child.'

Viviana gave a sharp intake of breath. 'You—'

Alessandro lifted one hand. 'Allow him to speak without interruptions.'

Viviana glowered, but to Dragan's relief she fell silent.

Dragan took a deep breath. Melinda's mother definitely wasn't going to like this next bit. But it had to be said. 'Thank you, Your Majesty.' He paused. 'I'm not asking for your permission to marry your daughter. I'm asking for your *blessing*.'

'My blessing?'

'It would mean a lot to Melinda—and to me. But if you choose to withhold your blessing, I will still marry her. Because we are meant to be together.'

Alessandro looked thoughtful. 'She is a princess. She is used to the finer things in life. Can you afford that?'

Dragan smiled. 'She has royal blood, but at heart Melinda is a country vet. I admit that I wouldn't be able to keep her in the kind of thing you have in mind—jewels and haute couture—but that's not what she wants anyway.'

'No?'

'No,' Dragan affirmed. 'I would have paid a year's salary for her engagement ring, if that's what she'd wanted—but I know Melinda. She'd have taken it back to the shop the next day, picked something much smaller, got a refund for the difference and given the money to an animal charity.'

Alessandro raised an eyebrow.

OK. So this was where he would be thrown out of the palace.

And then, to his surprise, Alessandro burst out laughing. 'That sounds like *exactly* what she would do. You know my daughter's heart, then.'

'Yes. And I can tell you now I will be a good husband. I'll love her and cherish her—and our children—for the rest of my days. Sometimes my hours are long but, then, so are Melinda's.'

'You expect her to work after your marriage—after the baby arrives?' Viviana asked sharply.

Dragan met her stare without flinching. 'I expect Melinda to do what makes her happy. She loves her job and she's very, very good at it. If she chooses to work full time or part time, she has my support. We'll work out what's best for us as a family.' He paused. 'And that's the most important thing— family. Without that, all the property in the world means nothing. You can't put a price on love.'

There was a long, long silence.

And then Alessandro nodded. 'My daughter says you are a good man. And we had you investigated.'

'You did what?' Melinda asked, sounding appalled.

'I did what any father would do. I found out just who the man was who wanted to take my daughter—to see if he will make her happy.' He inclined his head towards Dragan. 'You worked to make sure your family's honour remained intact before you left Croatia. And you went to England with nothing—took nothing, expected nothing, and you have worked hard to make a good life. You are a man of honour. And I know you love my daughter. So, yes, you have my blessing.'

Melinda stood up and took Dragan's hand, then looked at her mother. 'And yours, *Mamma*?'

'You should have been queen,' Viviana said, shaking her head. 'But you have always known what you wanted to do. And if your father is happy to give his blessing, I will not stand in your way.'

'Families are important,' Dragan said softly again. 'And we have something for you.' He glanced at Melinda, who took three small envelopes from her handbag and handed one to each of her parents and her sister.

'What is this?' Viviana asked.

'I think I know,' Serena said with a broad smile. 'Open yours first, *Mamma*.'

Viviana frowned, but did so. Opened the card. And her eyes widened as she took in exactly what was inside the card.

The picture from Melinda's scan.

'The first photograph of your grandchild,' Dragan said. 'And I would like very much to know that our son or daughter will have a *nonno* and *nonna* who will come to visit.' He smiled at Serena. 'I know already our children will have an aunt in a million.'

Serena turned bright pink, stood up and hugged him. '*Grazie*, Dragan. And welcome to our family.'

Then Viviana shocked him completely by doing the same.

'My daughter is right. Welcome to our family. I know you have no family, Dragan, so *il bambino* may only have one set of grandparents—but we will do our best to be as good as two.'

CHAPTER FIFTEEN

BACK in Penhally, Dragan brought a tray of cold drinks and biscuits through to the living room, where Melinda, Lauren and Chloe were talking non-stop.

'I'm leaving you lot to it,' he said. 'I'm taking Bramble out—but I'll have my phone on if you need me.' He gave Melinda a lingering kiss. '*Ciao, tesoro.*' He whistled to Bramble, and a few moments later Melinda heard the front door close.

'I asked you both over tonight for a reason,' she said to Lauren and Chloe. 'You know I'm getting married at the end of the month…well, I need bridesmaids. Which is where you come in.'

'You want *us* as your bridesmaids?' Chloe asked, looking shocked.

Melinda rolled her eyes. 'I wouldn't have asked you if I didn't.'

Lauren looked worried. 'I don't know, Melinda. I'd hate it if I tripped over your train or something and fell flat on my face in the middle of the aisle. You know how clumsy I am. I don't want to spoil your wedding.'

'And you're a princess, Melinda. It's a royal wedding.' Chloe bit her lip. 'I can't be a royal bridesmaid.'

'Yes, you can. Because it's not a royal wedding, it's *my* wedding,' Melinda reminded them. 'We need to get a few things straight here. Lauren, you *won't* fall flat on your face in the aisle. You can wear flat shoes and the dress can be ballerina-length if that'll make you feel more comfortable. Look, you two are my best friends. I really want you as my bridesmaids, along with my sister. And my wedding day just won't be the same if you're not.'

Chloe and Lauren eyed each other doubtfully.

'If you're sure…' Lauren began.

She hugged them each in turn. 'Of course I'm sure. And I hope you realise you're top of our godmother list, too. Along with my sister Serena, or she'll have us thrown in the dungeons.' As her friends' eyes widened, she laughed. 'Figuratively speaking. I think it's actually against the law for her to chuck anyone in the dungeons. She just likes saying it. Anyway, I'm under instructions to measure you tonight for the dresses.'

'So we're not going shopping?' Lauren asked.

'Yes and no,' Melinda said. 'Serena has this friend who's a brilliant dressmaker. She's emailed me half a dozen designs—we pick the ones we like and her friend makes them, then comes over for the fitting. We get to choose colours, too.'

'I've never had a dress made just for me,' Chloe said quietly.

'Nor me,' Lauren said.

'Well, now's your chance. And it'll be by someone who Serena reckons is going to be one of the hottest designers in Milan by next summer.'

'You're really sure about this?' Lauren asked.

'Absolutely.' Melinda fetched her laptop from her briefcase. 'Let's sort out our dresses.'

Later that evening, Melinda was aware that Dragan had gone really quiet. 'What's wrong?' she asked.

'I was thinking about the wedding.'

She went cold. 'Have you changed your mind?'

'No, of course not.' He hugged her. 'It's just that tonight you were sorting out bridesmaid stuff. And that reminded me, it's traditional for the groom to have a best man.' He looked away. 'I always thought I'd be my brother's best man at his wedding, and he would be mine.'

Melinda stroked the hair back from his face. 'Oh, *zlato*. I'm sorry.'

'Not your fault.' He sighed. 'But it leaves me with a problem. I have no family. And I don't know who to ask.'

'What about Nick Tremayne?'

'Nick?' Dragan looked surprised.

'He's your friend as well as your colleague, isn't he?'

'We're not that close…but you're probably right. Nick would be a good choice.'

'Then ask him, *caro*.'

The following morning, before surgery, Dragan knocked on Nick's door, opened it and leant against the jamb. 'A word?'

The senior partner looked up from his desk. 'That's my line.'

'I know.' Dragan coughed. 'Nick, I need a favour.'

'What sort of favour?'

'I'm getting married. And I need someone I can trust to hold the ring for me and make a half-decent speech at the reception.'

Nick's brown eyes widened. 'Hang on. You're asking me to be your best man?'

'Got it in one.'

'Good lord.' Nick smiled, and suddenly looked younger than Dragan had seen him for a long, long time. 'I'd be delighted. Thank you.'

'Good. Oh, there is one tiny little thing.'

Nick's voice was full of suspicion. 'What?'

'I'd rather you didn't bring Cruella as your wedding guest.'

Nick's frown deepened. 'Why?'

'She's upset half the people in the practice—Kate, Alison, Hazel. She's rude about my dog. And she was rude to Melinda before she realised that she was speaking to Princess Melinda Fortesque—since then, she's been driving Melinda crazy, trying to be pally with her and swapping fashion tips. I can't get through to her that Melinda hates all this royal stuff.'

'Ah.' Nick grimaced.

'I don't want an atmosphere at the wedding. Melinda's mother is, um…' Dragan searched for a diplomatic expression '…a strong character. And if someone wasn't particularly careful about what she said or who might overhear her, it could make life difficult.'

'Point taken,' Nick said. 'I'll come on my own. Actually, I think Natasha's planning on going back to Rock anyway.'

Dragan knew a few people who'd correct that to 'crawling back under the rock she came from', but held his tongue. 'Thank you.'

The last days of the month sped by. Serena came over from Contarini to help with the wedding plans, and Dragan was impressed by how quickly and easily the future queen of Contarini managed to organise everything and took all the stress off Melinda—and at the same time she still managed to make the bride feel that she was completely in control. Melinda simply said what she wanted and Serena organised it.

Serena also had things to say about the press.

'If we have a deal with syndicated rights, we get a wedding photographer who's desperate to take the best pictures of his life, and you'll get a measure of privacy—well, as much as any royal wedding will. The papers will be happy because they get brilliant pictures, and the paparazzi won't hassle us because the deal is done and dusted. Everybody wins.'

'And for syndicated rights, we get money,' Melinda said thoughtfully. 'Which I'd like to donate to charity.'

'You took the words out of my mouth,' Serena said. 'Do you have anything special in mind?'

'Local ones who do animal rescue, plus something towards church funds,' Melinda said.

'And the primary school and village nursery,' Dragan added. 'They could do with some new play equipment.'

'And something to the lifeboats,' Melinda said.

'Good idea,' Dragan said. 'Kate, one of the midwives at our practice, was married to the man who ran the lifeboat station. He died in a rescue at sea—and Nick, the senior partner at my practice, lost his father and brother in the rescue too.'

'I read about that. Such a tragedy.' Serena looked serious. 'Right. Give me a list of contacts and I'll sort it out.'

'You're going to be an excellent head of state,' Dragan told her. 'You've got the right touch with people.'

'Melinda's good with people, too,' Serena pointed out.

'But her heart wouldn't have been in the job, so it wouldn't have been right for her. Whereas you—you'll make an excellent queen because your heart is in it.'

'And my sister's heart is with you.' She smiled. 'And so it should be. I know you're right for her.'

'You thrive on all this wheeling and dealing, don't you?' Melinda asked with a smile.

Serena grinned. 'You bet I do. And this wedding is going to be a day the whole of Penhally's going to remember for a long, long time—with a lot of love and affection.'

On the Saturday morning, Dragan woke early. It felt odd not to have Melinda curled in bed beside him, but there had been much insistence from both Melinda and Serena on sticking to tradition. According to them, it was bad luck to see the bride on the day until she arrived at the church, so Melinda and Serena had spent the night at Chloe's house.

He went over to the window and peered out. It was a perfect spring day, with the sun shining and the sky a rich deep blue.

His wedding day.

There was just one shadow in his heart—that his family weren't there to share the day with him. But Melinda's words echoed in his head. *Your family will be there in spirit.*

'I hope so,' he said softly. 'Because I miss you so much. But I'll see you in my children's faces. And your love still goes on in my heart.'

He drove Bramble over to Lizzie Chamberlain's. 'I think Melinda would've liked her at the wedding,' he confided to Lizzie.

Lizzie laughed. 'You can imagine what kind of chaos a flattie would cause at a wedding—they like to be the centre of attention. Don't you, girl?' she said, bending down to cuddle Bramble. 'What you and Melinda did—donating that money—thank you. It's going to make a real difference to the rescue work,' she said.

'That's what we wanted,' Dragan said simply. 'We're part of this community.'

'That you most certainly are,' Lizzie said feelingly. 'Have you got time for a cup of tea?'

'Make that coffee, and you're on,' Dragan said with a smile. 'And while I'm here, I can have a chat with your mum about how it's going with the new drugs and exercise routine.'

Lizzie tutted. 'It's your wedding day. You're not supposed to be working.'

'You'll be doing me a favour,' he said. 'Keeping me busy so I don't have time to think or get nervous.'

Lizzie tapped the side of her nose. 'Got you.'

Meanwhile, at Chloe's house, the wedding preparations were going ahead at full steam. Vicky had come over to do the bride's and bridesmaids' hair and make-up. At first she'd been a little overawed by the thought of being official hair-dresser and beautician to two of the Contarini royal family, but as soon as she'd met Serena she was back to being her normal chatterbox self.

'Doorbell!' Lauren yelled. 'Want me to get it, Chloe?'

Chloe, who was busy making yet another round of tea, put her head round the door. 'Isn't a bit early for the flowers?'

'You stay put,' Serena warned Melinda. 'Vicky, stick pins in her if she moves. And if that's Dragan I'll shut the door so they don't see each other.'

Lauren walked back into the living room a few minutes later, carrying a single red rose. 'Not Dragan. But I'd guess this is from him,' she said, handing the rose to Melinda.

Melinda opened the card and read the message. *Six hours until you make my life complete.*

'Oh-h-h,' she breathed.

Serena grabbed the card and read it. 'Don't cry. You'll smudge the make-up.'

'It's waterproof,' Vicky chipped in.

'Don't give her the excuse.' Serena shook her head impatiently. 'And, Lini, I can read your face like a book. You can't go and see him. It's bad luck.'

'To *see* him, yes.' Melinda grabbed her mobile phone. 'It doesn't mean I can't talk to him.'

'It's bad luck,' Serena insisted.

Melinda sighed and put the phone away.

But when a second rose arrived an hour later—and another one an hour after that—Melinda grabbed her phone again. 'I need to talk to him.' When Serena was about to protest, she said softly, 'I have my friends and family around me. Dragan's on his own, once he's taken Bramble over to Lizzie's.'

Serena sighed. All right. 'Leave this to me.'

* * *

A few minutes later, Dragan opened the door and his eyes widened in surprise when he saw Serena there. 'Is Melinda all right?'

'Yes, but I have a message from her.'

He went cold. 'You'd better come in.' He closed the door behind her. Please, don't let this all go wrong now. He could barely force the question out. 'She's changed her mind?'

'*Idiota*! Of course she hasn't. But it's bad luck for the bride and groom to see each other before church, and...' Serena flapped an impatient hand. 'She says she loves you and she loves the red roses—and she's counting the minutes until she's your bride.' She gave him a hug. 'That was such a romantic thing to do.'

'There should be two more. We're on a countdown,' Dragan said.

'That's so *sweet*.' She paused. 'And, actually, there was something I wanted to say, too. When you marry Melinda, she'll be your family—but so will I. And *Mamma* and *Papà*. My father really likes you, you know.'

The lump in his throat was so big he couldn't say a word. He just hugged her right back.

'I'll see you in church,' she said. 'And just so you don't worry, Melinda will be precisely three minutes late.' She smiled. 'It's tradition. If she had her way, she'd be three minutes early!'

And finally everything was ready. The flowers had arrived, along with one last rose from Dragan. Everyone's hair and make-up was pristine, and Vicky had gone to get changed for church.

And then the doorbell went.

Serena glanced at her watch. 'That must be *Mamma* and *Papà*, with the cars. Ready?'

'Ready,' Melinda said softly.

Chloe answered the door and did as much of a curtsey as she could in her bridesmaid's dress. 'Your Majesty.'

'You must be...Chloe? Lauren?' Viviana asked.

'Chloe.'

'Serena has told me what a good friend you are to my daughter. *Grazie, tesoro.*'

'Um, my pleasure,' Chloe said, looking slightly awestruck.

Viviana swept in. 'And you are Lauren, yes?'

'Yes, Your Majesty.' Lauren also curtseyed, and nearly tripped.

Viviana took her arm for support. 'No more curtseys.' She surveyed the four women. 'You look lovely.' She came to stand in front of Melinda. 'And you...*mia bambina. Che bellissima,*' she said softly.

'Stop it, *Mamma.* You'll make her cry and spoil her make-up. Hormones,' Serena reminded her swiftly. 'And that goes for you too, *Papà*—you only say things to make Melinda smile. Now, we must all go to the church and wait for Melinda just inside the lych-gate.'

'Bossy,' Alessandro grumbled, but he was smiling.

When the girls had left, he took Melinda's hand. 'You look beautiful, Melinda,' he said, 'and I am very proud of you. You are a true royal because you always stand up for what you believe in—and your Dragan is a good man. I am proud to give you away to him, and to know he will treat you as the heart of his heart.' And then he looked worried. 'Please, no tears. Serena is scarier than your mother.'

She didn't think he meant it—not quite—but it made her smile.

'Shall we go?' he asked.

She locked the door behind her and gave the key to her father for safekeeping and transfer back to Chloe during the reception. He helped her into the vintage Rolls-Royce convertible outside, and they slowly made their way to the church. People seemed to be lined up all the way along Harbour Road, throwing flowers and confetti.

Alessandro raised an eyebrow. 'Weren't you and Serena banning confetti?'

'This is biodegradable,' Melinda explained with a smile. 'And we've said we want the bird-seed type in the church grounds.'

Alessandro laughed. 'You've thought of everything.'

He helped her out of the car when they reached the church and ushered her through the lych-gate. Serena, Chloe and Lauren were all there, holding their bouquets.

Just before Alessandro gave Melinda her bouquet, Viviana hugged her. 'I wish you so much happiness, *figlia mia*,' she said.

'*Grazie*.' Melinda could hardly speak for the threatening tears.

'*Mamma*! Church, now,' Serena ordered. 'Go and give Reverend Kenner the nod that we are ready.'

Viviana gave her younger daughter a speaking look, but did as requested.

'Deep breath. And smile,' Serena directed. 'You're going to marry the man you love.'

And then Melinda walked through the church door on her father's arm, with her bridesmaids behind her, to the strains of 'Jesu, Joy of Man's Desiring'.

She glanced around quickly. The church was absolutely packed—standing room only. And she knew absolutely everyone there. They'd all come to wish her and Dragan luck and love and happiness.

As she passed the front pews, she saw her mother, her Uncle Benito and a space for her father—and behind them she recognised more aunts and uncles and cousins. The entire royal family of Contarini had turned out—how on earth had Serena done this without her so much as guessing? And there were all the friends she and Dragan shared from Penhally.

And then Dragan turned and smiled at her, his dark eyes full of love—and nothing else mattered.

The music stopped, and then Reverend Kenner was smiling at them both. 'Dearly beloved, we are gathered here today…'

0108 Gen Std HB

™ MILLS & BOON®

Pure reading pleasure

FEBRUARY 2008 HARDBACK TITLES

ROMANCE

The Italian Billionaire's Pregnant Bride *Lynne Graham*	978 0 263 20238 0
The Guardian's Forbidden Mistress *Miranda Lee*	978 0 263 20239 7
Secret Baby, Convenient Wife *Kim Lawrence*	978 0 263 20240 3
Caretti's Forced Bride *Jennie Lucas*	978 0 263 20241 0
The Salvatore Marriage Deal *Natalie Rivers*	978 0 263 20242 7
The British Billionaire Affair *Susanne James*	978 0 263 20243 4
One-Night Love-Child *Anne McAllister*	978 0 263 20244 1
Virgin: Wedded at the Italian's Convenience *Diana Hamilton*	978 0 263 20245 8
The Bride's Baby *Liz Fielding*	978 0 263 20246 5
Expecting a Miracle *Jackie Braun*	978 0 263 20247 2
Wedding Bells at Wandering Creek *Patricia Thayer*	978 0 263 20248 9
The Loner's Guarded Heart *Michelle Douglas*	978 0 263 20249 6
Sweetheart Lost and Found *Shirley Jump*	978 0 263 20250 2
The Single Dad's Patchwork Family *Claire Baxter*	978 0 263 20251 9
His Island Bride *Marion Lennox*	978 0 263 20252 6
Desert Prince, Expectant Mother *Olivia Gates*	978 0 263 20253 3

HISTORICAL

Lady Gwendolen Investigates *Anne Ashley*	978 0 263 20189 5
The Unknown Heir *Anne Herries*	978 0 263 20190 1
Forbidden Lord *Helen Dickson*	978 0 263 20191 8

MEDICAL™

The Doctor's Royal Love-Child *Kate Hardy*	978 0 263 19867 6
A Consultant Beyond Compare *Joanna Neil*	978 0 263 19871 3
The Surgeon Boss's Bride *Melanie Milburne*	978 0 263 19875 1
A Wife Worth Waiting For *Maggie Kingsley*	978 0 263 19879 9

Pure reading pleasure

FEBRUARY 2008 LARGE PRINT TITLES

ROMANCE

The Greek Tycoon's Virgin Wife *Helen Bianchin*	978 0 263 20018 8
Italian Boss, Housekeeper Bride *Sharon Kendrick*	978 0 263 20019 5
Virgin Bought and Paid For *Robyn Donald*	978 0 263 20020 1
The Italian Billionaire's Secret Love-Child *Cathy Williams*	978 0 263 20021 8
The Mediterranean Rebel's Bride *Lucy Gordon*	978 0 263 20022 5
Found: Her Long-Lost Husband *Jackie Braun*	978 0 263 20023 2
The Duke's Baby *Rebecca Winters*	978 0 263 20024 9
Millionaire to the Rescue *Ally Blake*	978 0 263 20025 6

HISTORICAL

Masquerading Mistress *Sophia James*	978 0 263 20121 5
Married By Christmas *Anne Herries*	978 0 263 20125 3
Taken By the Viking *Michelle Styles*	978 0 263 20129 1

MEDICAL™

The Italian GP's Bride *Kate Hardy*	978 0 263 19932 1
The Consultant's Italian Knight *Maggie Kingsley*	978 0 263 19933 8
Her Man of Honour *Melanie Milburne*	978 0 263 19934 5
One Special Night... *Margaret McDonagh*	978 0 263 19935 2
The Doctor's Pregnancy Secret *Leah Martyn*	978 0 263 19936 9
Bride for a Single Dad *Laura Iding*	978 0 263 19937 6

0108 Gen Std LP

0208 Gen Std HB

MARCH 2008 HARDBACK TITLES

ROMANCE

The Markonos Bride *Michelle Reid*	978 0 263 20254 0
The Italian's Passionate Revenge *Lucy Gordon*	978 0 263 20255 7
The Greek Tycoon's Baby Bargain *Sharon Kendrick*	978 0 263 20256 4
Di Cesare's Pregnant Mistress *Chantelle Shaw*	978 0 263 20257 1
The Billionaire's Virgin Mistress *Sandra Field*	978 0 263 20258 8
At the Sicilian Count's Command *Carole Mortimer*	978 0 263 20259 5
Blackmailed For Her Baby *Elizabeth Power*	978 0 263 20260 1
The Cattle Baron's Virgin Wife *Lindsay Armstrong*	978 0 263 20261 8
His Pregnant Housekeeper *Caroline Anderson*	978 0 263 20262 5
The Italian Playboy's Secret Son *Rebecca Winters*	978 0 263 20263 2
Her Sheikh Boss *Carol Grace*	978 0 263 20264 9
Wanted: White Wedding *Natasha Oakley*	978 0 263 20265 6
The Heir's Convenient Wife *Myrna Mackenzie*	978 0 263 20266 3
Coming Home to the Cattleman *Judy Christenberry*	978 0 263 20267 0
Billionaire Doctor, Ordinary Nurse *Carol Marinelli*	978 0 263 20268 7
The Sheikh Surgeon's Baby *Meredith Webber*	978 0 263 20269 4

HISTORICAL

The Last Rake In London *Nicola Cornick*	978 0 263 20192 5
The Outrageous Lady Felsham *Louise Allen*	978 0 263 20193 2
An Unconventional Miss *Dorothy Elbury*	978 0 263 20194 9

MEDICAL™

Nurse Bride, Bayside Wedding *Gill Sanderson*	978 0 263 19883 6
The Outback Doctor's Surprise Bride *Amy Andrews*	978 0 263 19887 4
A Wedding at Limestone Coast *Lucy Clark*	978 0 263 19888 1
The Doctor's Meant-To-Be Marriage *Janice Lynn*	978 0 263 19889 8

MILLS & BOON®

Pure reading pleasure

0208 Gen Std LP

MARCH 2008 LARGE PRINT TITLES

ROMANCE

The Billionaire's Captive Bride *Emma Darcy*	978 0 263 20026 3
Bedded, or Wedded? *Julia James*	978 0 263 20027 0
The Boss's Christmas Baby *Trish Morey*	978 0 263 20028 7
The Greek Tycoon's Unwilling Wife *Kate Walker*	978 0 263 20029 4
Winter Roses *Diana Palmer*	978 0 263 20030 0
The Cowboy's Christmas Proposal *Judy Christenberry*	978 0 263 20031 7
Appointment at the Altar *Jessica Hart*	978 0 263 20032 4
Caring for His Baby *Caroline Anderson*	978 0 263 20033 1

HISTORICAL

Scandalous Lord, Rebellious Miss *Deb Marlowe*	978 0 263 20133 8
The Duke's Gamble *Miranda Jarrett*	978 0 263 20137 6
The Damsel's Defiance *Meriel Fuller*	978 0 263 20141 3

MEDICAL™

The Single Dad's Marriage Wish *Carol Marinelli*	978 0 263 19938 3
The Playboy Doctor's Proposal *Alison Roberts*	978 0 263 19939 0
The Consultant's Surprise Child *Joanna Neil*	978 0 263 19940 6
Dr Ferrero's Baby Secret *Jennifer Taylor*	978 0 263 19941 3
Their Very Special Child *Dianne Drake*	978 0 263 19942 0
The Surgeon's Runaway Bride *Olivia Gates*	978 0 263 19943 7